Brindle 24

———

The Last Day
in the
Life of a Town

J.J.Brown

This book is inspired by actual events. The names and characters are the product of the author's imagination or are used fictitiously. Any resemblance to people, living or dead, is entirely coincidental.

Brindle 24

Contents

Author's Note

Writing Brindle 24, I was inspired by the brave people who shared their experiences about the impact of gas drilling on their lives. They are farmers, singers, poets, physicians and scientists who exercised their freedom of expression. I thank them.

My gratitude goes to Susanna Rosensteel for editing and to Florencio Ares for book cover design.

Dedicated to the memory of Upton Sinclair.

"One way to open your eyes is to ask yourself, 'What if I had never seen this before? What if I knew I would never see it again?'"

— Rachel Carson

Prologue

The town of Brindle is close to where I was born and raised, at the northern end of the rock formation known as the Marcellus Shale. No more than a few thousand people live here. This is the story of some of Brindle's families—Beth Smith and her parents, the orphan twins Mark and Matt, Adrian Berger and his father Henry, and Officer Joe—over the course of one day.

8 AM

Officer Joe wakes up from a recurring nightmare of falling into a chasm on fire, near a hill rocked by explosions. He bolts out of bed in a sweat, gasping for air and looking for the rest of his squad. He focuses his eyes on his digital alarm clock. It blinks red. He listens to it beep steadily beside him, the only sound in the room, while he brings his breathing back under control. Sunlight streams around the window shades and grounds him; this is morning and he's in Brindle, not Afghanistan. He's home. He gets up and opens the shades. The sun is burning the fog off the ground and wisps linger in the hollows.

A mile from Officer Joe's place, an unmarked white tanker rumbles along the narrow pavement of Route 32 at the crossroads. Seconds later, a flatbed trailer carrying a bulldozer follows the tanker. An electric car idles, waiting to cross at the intersection of Route 32 and Smith's Lane. Adrian Berger, a year out of high school, is in the passenger seat and his father is driving. Each time the road clears, their small red car advances a few feet. Another truck appears and blocks the way. A gas truck, followed by water trucks, trucks marked with yellow and black hazard signs—the stream of traffic never ends. Their car rolls back.

Adrian squints. "These guys all work with you up here?"

His father, Henry Berger, is an anxious person. He repeats a phrase over and over in his mind: *the things people say*.

"They work at the same gas drilling site, yes, but not with me, exactly," he says. "They're in construction, I'm in sampling." *The things people say*, he echoes mindlessly to himself. None of the phrases he finds himself repeating at times mean anything at all to him. He doesn't even know why he says them. He knows why he thinks them, because he can't control his thoughts.

He sees a gray squirrel at the side of the road right next to them. Poised ready to bolt across the road, the tiny animal twitches a long feathery tail. Henry wonders how the animal figures out when to cross; vibrations from the road's surface, he imagines.

Henry is a scientist, an expert consultant to companies in the energy industry. His position is not the same as when he was a full-time employee. Now he consults for several companies, and this work pays better. He likes being a consultant. It prevents him from becoming too attached to any one of the companies. The big workplaces have a way of morphing a human personality into a specialized machine. Along with the inevitable overuse of company jargon, the work itself becomes soul-numbing, unbearably boring; testing soil samples, writing reports, meeting with managers to explain the findings. Even though Henry is not completely in control of himself, he doesn't like the idea of anyone or anything else controlling him. Consulting suits him.

Adrian assumes that his father, who he came up with from Brooklyn for the week, and all these truckers probably do work together. Adrian doesn't understand his father's work. He doesn't have to understand it. Years lie ahead of him for all of that. Someday he will be forced to stop stalling, stop fooling around, and start thinking about money. That day has not yet come. He is simply grateful to his father for letting him push back life's hard decisions a few years.

When Adrian graduated from Bronx High School of Science last year without a plan, they were both relieved that he graduated at all. Spending the week together all the way out here in Brindle seems perfect to both of them.

A public-school bus rolls up to the intersection and comes to a stop right across from Adrian and Henry on Smith's Lane. Adrian thinks these kids are lucky. No taking the subway to school here.

Chemical trucks, water tankers, flatbeds loaded with drilling equipment file along in an endless river of traffic, preventing Adrian and his father from crossing the road. Adrian wonders whether the truck drivers are as insanely frustrated with their job as he used to be with his commute. He took three subway trains from Brooklyn every day to get to Bronx Science and then the same route back, day after day, over an hour each way, all four years of high school.

"Squirrel," Adrian says.

Henry looks for the animal at the side of the road. Still waiting, it stands motionless with one front paw raised.

Adrian hums a song he heard last night. After a few repeats, he remembers the words. He sings softly, "Water, water, you can't drink gasoline. Hmm, hmm...water, water."

"Where's that from?" Henry asks.

"YouTube."

"No, I mean, where. Geographically." YouTube doesn't mean anything at all to Henry. "YouTube" is just another one of the meaningless things people say.

"Right. It's from the Karoo, South Africa," Adrian answers.

"Ah," Henry says, and he is surprised. He looks over at his son, studying his posture, the way he holds his hands, his facial expression too, in a futile attempt to discover what he's thinking. "The Karoo." This is not one of the things people usually say.

Adrian imagines that coming up here could be a kind of research project of his own. Not for science, like his father's work, but for background on song lyrics—new ideas to bring back to the city with him. The trip could be something like work, for a budding artist.

You have to live in order to have something to write about, his English teacher had said.

Getting close to more natural, country people up here should be good for realism. Sitting in his father's car at the edge of the road and waiting for a chance to cross, Adrian thinks he probably has to suffer. Yes, he'll have to suffer in some way he hasn't yet, in order to have something interesting to write about. Then he'll sing about suffering. All the singers he admired did.

He starts to lower his window for fresh air.

Henry says, "I wouldn't. Exhaust fumes from the trucks. The air isn't good for the lungs."

Adrian lets out an exaggerated sigh and closes the window. This is not what he was expecting out of a trip to the country. He taps his fingers on his thighs and sings, "Water, clean water, you can't drink gasoline. Water, water..."

Henry thinks he'll go mad listening—that is, if he is not insane already. The song repeats in his head: *Water, clean water*. He can't tell his son to shut up, but he wishes he could.

Directly across the road from Henry and Adrian, two young men in a pickup truck also wait to cross over Route 32 on Smith's Lane. Their truck idles behind the school bus. They are twins. Their long, ash blonde hair is covered with matching black knit caps.

The driver curses at a water tanker truck as it approaches them. "Said we wouldn't even notice them," he says. The tanker passes.

His twin snorts. "Maybe they were talking about themselves; they wouldn't even notice us. They don't notice us. Do they? No. No, they do not."

"Made me late twice this week." The driver leans on his horn and lets out a string of curses as he watches an 18-wheeler roll by.

"That was creative."

"Shut up. If I sat here all day and I counted all the trucks, no one would believe me."

"I counted them one day. It's a convoy," his brother says. He bursts out laughing, "Con-voy. What a weird word."

Children and teens stretch their arms and heads out of the school bus windows. They call out to the twins in the pickup truck. The children are laughing and reaching; some are screaming. A mile and a half down the road and seven minutes later they will be students again. For now, they are free to play with abandon on the bus. Summer recess is only five days away and the children are bursting out of their daily confinement.

The older woman behind the wheel of the yellow bus drives part-time. Driving is good work and steady, predictable pay. The job gets her out of the house and helps take care of some of the bills, like water and electricity. She looks over the top of her glasses, trying to see farther down the road. Glasses or no glasses, she can't see as well as she used to. Every day is the same thing; she has to wait for a space between the passing trucks. She cautiously puts the bus in gear. Her heart races like a wild rabbit pursued by a dog.

A fleeting thought runs through her mind, of taking the medication to regulate her heart rhythm. She can't remember whether she took her pills this morning. The paths laid down long ago in her memory are polished with time. But not the imprints of more recent events, no; they disappear nearly as soon as they arise, vanishing like morning fog in the summer heat. She remembers every note, every word of the church songs without even looking at the hymnal when she plays the pipe organ for the choir on Sunday mornings. But her thoughts have become like water vapor. She cannot remember what she did or didn't do yesterday, or even this morning. Old age, she imagines. The levels of oxygen that enter her brain have been reduced by the blockage along her blood vessels, lined with the damage and residue of many years.

The school bus rolls forward slowly and she gives it more gas.

Waiting at the crossroads in their electric car, Adrian and his father both want to take advantage of this opportunity and get moving.

The squirrel makes a mad dash across the road.

"Oh! Look, he made it," Adrian says.

Henry hesitates. "I can't see," he frets.

"Go for it. They set you up," Adrian urges him on. "They set you a pick."

The things people say, Henry thinks. What do the words even mean? He isn't sure. A pick. A sports reference? Yes, it is a game. Basketball. That's it. You block so your partner can score.

As Adrian and Henry's car rolls forward slowly, the front of the school bus approaches. For a moment, it seems they will both finally get to cross. Adrian sees a tanker coming around the bend heading right for the car.

"Back up!" Adrian panics. He reaches across his father's arm and hits the horn repeatedly.

The bus continues forward like a deaf-mute dinosaur.

The tanker swerves right. It hits the bus with a glancing blow and continues plowing along the road.

Adrian yells.

The tanker's impact pushes the rear of the school bus sideways. The metal groans, the bus tips slowly. The bus falls over on its side, off the road.

Children pile over one another, shrieking. They climb out the windows, fall to the gravel and grass, swarm along the shoulder of the road.

More trucks flow past, swerving to avoid the accident.

Henry is struck dumb. He slowly backs his car off the road. Before they come to a stop, his son jumps out of the car and runs to the chaos. Henry, speechless, watches him go. Children surround Adrian, clamoring all at once. Others are crying where they sit on the grass behind the toppled bus. A small boy stands beside the bus door. He is screaming like a siren.

"No, no, don't cry. Don't worry. Help's on the way," Adrian says. He sees a little girl, her face wet from a bloody nose, her hands covering her eyes.

He pulls out his cell phone and dials 9-1-1. "Emergency. *Christ!* What? It's an accident, bus full of kids. I'm in...Dad! Where are we?"

Henry gets out of the car. "Brindle." He walks to the children, speaking quietly to them. "It's alright. Someone is coming. Don't cry. Call home..." But in his head he hears, *it's a disaster, no one will help them. Go home. It's a disaster.*

"I'm in Brindle," Adrian says on the phone and he looks up at a road sign. "Route 32. What? Adrian, Adrian Berger."

He hyperventilates. A tall, thin girl stares at him. She points to the front of the bus where it landed on its side. Adrian sees that the old driver is slumped sideways. She is motionless. The boy standing by the bus door hasn't stopped screaming. He's getting hoarse.

*****

Officer Joe gets the call about the bus accident when he's on the road passing by the school. He's a few miles away. He turns his vehicle around, puts on the siren, and speeds back to Route 32. He's going to block off traffic until the accident is cleared up there. They told him on the call that the town's volunteer ambulance was already on the way with two med techs.

The tanker that hit the bus pulls off the road and slows to a stop, fifty yards farther down on the shoulder. Trucks keep surging by in an uninterrupted stream.

Adrian feels a wave of energy. He knows it's rage. He darts across the road and sprints all the way to the tanker cab. He springs up, pounding on the driver's door. The driver leans away, looking dazed.

"You think you own the road? Idiot!" Adrian yells, "Get out. Get out!"

The twins in the pickup truck pull over behind him. They climb out and race to the tanker. Pushing Adrian aside, they wrench the truck cab door open. Pummeling the truck driver, they pull him to the ground and kneel over him.

The driver raises his hands in the air helplessly. "I couldn't stop. I couldn't." He begins to cry. He hears the volunteer ambulance approaching before he sees it. The siren wails, getting closer.

"Did I kill anybody?" the truck driver asks.

Out of breath, the twins back away from him without answering. They leave him lying there spitting blood and they turn on Adrian.

"Who the hell are you?" The taller brother steps closer.

"Are you with him?" The other twin nods toward the tanker driver cowering on the ground behind them.

"No! No," Adrian says. He guesses that they are a year or two younger than he is, but they're taller, lean, and fit. They smell of weed and coffee. He is afraid.

He points toward his father. "I'm with him."

The twins look over at the group of crying schoolchildren clustered around a tall, wiry man. They recognize Henry Berger. He's the man who comes to see about fixing the water problems in Brindle.

"The science guy? Then you *are* with them!" One of the brothers pushes Adrian backward. The three fall to the ground, wrestling in the gravel on the road's shoulder.

Officer Joe drives toward the tanker and turns off his siren. He slows his vehicle down and pulls over behind the fight. His military state of mind kicks in, like it always does in emergencies.

"Go home! Get out of here!" he yells through the open window, unbuckling his seatbelt. He gets out and towers over the twins, bellowing, "Get out of here. Get to school. Matt! Mark! You got a week left. Don't screw it up. Go!"

He watches the brothers lope away and then looks over the damage, sizing up Adrian. "You're all in one piece? Nothing broken?" Joe is surprised to see that his friend, the scientist, brought his son up here with him.

The trucker whines behind them. "Look what they did to me..." and he tries to clean his face where he's bleeding.

"Maybe you did it to yourself when you hit the school bus. That's what I think. What do you think?" Officer Joe says, without even looking back at him.

The trucker cries silently. He's injured, he doesn't know what happened to the children, and he's sure he'll lose his job.

Adrian feels the officer staring at him and reaches instinctively to cover a small pipe and plastic bag in the right front pocket of his jeans. He says, "I'm fine, really. But the bus—"

"Go on over there and help your father, if you can. He'll be shook up."

"Right."

Officer Joe looks at the line of trucks backed up where the road is closed now. The fallout from the accident will be a mess for everyone, he thinks—the energy company and the town too.

"Med techs are there; they'll see about the kids." Joe nods toward the truck driver, who tries to sit up and clutches one of his legs. "I'll take care of this one."

Adrian seems to be frozen in place.

"Go, I said!"

9 AM

Beth looks into her mother's darkened bedroom on the first floor of their home. "Maman, are you awake?" she asks. She walks into the room. The scents of old fruit and lavender perfume linger there. She wants to open a window. She can just make out that Maman is sitting motionless at her writing desk.

"I buried a baby bird under the rose bush this morning. A tiny one, still naked, no feathers. And later, I saw a sparrow on the fence," Beth says.

Maman nods silently, watching her daughter move through the room like an angel.

"She had food in her mouth. Going back and forth, looking. I think she was searching for the baby. I couldn't tell her," Beth says and she waits, remembering.

"Trying to feed her child," Maman says, as if there were nothing more important to her in the world.

Beth found the body lying in the dirt where it must have fallen from a nest. The birdling was small, no bigger than her thumb. The skin, translucent like wet ivory silk, stretched over the finest threads of veins. Baby birds fall from nests every year but she thinks she will never get used to seeing them like that. The flesh wrinkled in tiny folds around the pale yellow bill that was pressed closed in a final expression of disappointment. She wondered as she looked at the bird with its closed, gray eyes, *did your eyes ever open?*

She couldn't leave the body where insects would soon crawl over it. She used a sharp stone to dig the hole in the ground under the tall rose bush. The ground was wet. A long fern leaf went beneath the body as a bed. Another one on top was a covering. She filled in the dirt lightly over the burial site. When she finished, she marked the place with a round stone. But she doesn't talk about that part. The act was sacred, not something to be shared.

Now Beth opens the heavy, turquoise bedroom curtains to let in the morning sun.

"You buried her deep?" Maman asks.

"Six inches, about," Beth says as she makes up the bed.

Maman nods. "You know, you missed the school bus. I heard it go by."

Beth shrugs.

"Some time ago, wasn't it?"

"I can study here, Maman."

"What if you don't finish? *Ah, mon Dieu!* How many days are left?"

"Five. I'll read something at home. Don't worry." Beth lays a hand on her mother's arm gently and looks steadily into her eyes. "Look at me. Maman."

She waits for Maman to do it, to be sure she's listening. "I will catch up," Beth says slowly.

She scans the desk and shelves beside her mother's bed. The little urn of ashes from their pet cat's cremation is on the desk beside a candle and an open notebook. Piles of books are stacked differently than they were yesterday. Maman's been writing, and that's a good thing. From the bindings, Beth sees that the books are French, and not for the first time she reminds herself to learn French. Maybe this summer she will.

She leaves Maman's quiet room, goes outside, and sits behind the house. The ground is still wet with morning dew and the air carries the scent of new roses. The deep-red blossoms hang pendulous and pull down on thin stems. This air she inhales is rich, laden with oxygen given off by the plants that grow here behind the house and farther back in the fields and forests.

Respiration, breathing, is essential to all living things—she learned that at school this year. The life cycles in the environment carry oxygen to her by the air moving invisibly around and through all the things that breathe here in Brindle: plants, animals, and people. The atoms of oxygen come up from groundwater and into the plant roots and vessels, passing through the leaves and out into the air. This same oxygen is also inside of her, becoming part of her body—lungs, blood, cells, and DNA.

The many atoms that form Beth are connected to the air, water, and earth shared by everything and everyone here. She is part of that continuous life cycle. She imagines that the bird that died before eight in the morning today was also part of the cycle, the air and water and plants. These particles became part of the developing bird over the days of its life, particle by particle. In some way, the bird that died was Beth too. They are connected.

She would rather stay out here, observing, but she knows she has to finish this week of classes. She must pass in order to start high school in the fall. She must not fail. Maman and Da named her Elizabeth, "God's promise," Beth for short. She is their only child. She must go on, part of their family's life cycle.

Watching the small brown bird return and flit nervously back and forth along the wooden fence beside the rose brambles, Beth wishes she could speak "sparrow." She wonders, what would she tell the bird? She thinks it must be terrible to lose a baby. Would she try to comfort her or distract her? Would she show her the birdling burial site and tell her the story?

Beth goes back inside and fills a bucket with water from a large tank in the kitchen. The water is brought in from somewhere else every week. Water, like air, is made up of oxygen atoms too, oxygen and hydrogen, along with whatever came along with it from the source.

She's not sure what that might be. This water and this oxygen are not from Brindle, because here the oxygen cycle she learned about has been broken. This year in the spring, their water went bad.

She pulls on her heavy boots and carries the water bucket past the rose bushes, past the herb garden, and back to the barn behind the house. Her steps kick up the scents of herbs: thyme, mint, and lemon balm. The plants send up new stems each year from the roots that survived the winter and grew up again along the path. The perfumed walk is a mystical part of her world. Walking here is her favorite part of mornings. Sometimes, this is the highlight of her day.

Standing beside Maman's horse, listening to her drink, Beth thinks about what she has left to do by the end of the school week. The art project is finished. She has a final paper on the topic of her family heritage, for history class, one she hasn't started yet. She'll ask Maman later when she gets up—that is, *if* she gets up today. Some days she doesn't. An assignment for Beth's science class, on the living environment, remains to be tackled. That will be handed out today as the final project.

She learned all about the Marcellus Shale this year in science class. Rock made of clay and quartz was laid down four hundred million years ago. These layers hidden beneath their land fascinated her. Who knew four hundred million years had ever existed? Water covered the land here then, possibly saltwater, the books say, and that water was brimming with life. It was the age of fish. Whole continents were not formed then, not like they are now. Everything was different. She wonders whether this was the same time as when mythic gods and goddesses may have walked the earth, like Demeter, Persephone, and Hades— the ones that now are found only in constellations of stars and in story books.

Today, the black layers of shale wind along, thousands of feet below, dark serpents of rock underneath Brindle. Some believe that the shale holds an endless fortune—gas mined by the energy company. Older people are always searching for treasure, but she thinks they look in the wrong places. If they knew about her herb garden, the roses in bloom, and Maman's horse, Beth is certain people would value all these things. They would love them like she does when she sits behind her house, breathing, dreaming.

The horse finishes drinking her water and bangs her head against the bucket. Beth pats her on the side of the neck. She loves her.

Beth walks back to the house. A fossil rock she picked up from the stream last week is still outside the kitchen door. She placed it there as a mute sentry. The fossils could be from hundreds of millions of years ago, like the shale, she guesses, from the tiny sea creatures' outlines embedded in the rock.

She picks the rock up, heavy and cool in her palm. The fossil images lay next to one another. The mute, chalky white shell ridges are encased in deep gray sediment like a tomb around them. Maybe it was carbon atoms in their decaying compacted bodies that made the gas layer down there under the shale. She wonders whether the baby bird skeleton or her own will look like that one day, laying side by side, crushed and chalky white.

She wishes that the little fossil creatures could talk. What was it like here then, when water covered their hills?

Beth leaves her boots by the back door of the house. She sets a teapot full of filtered water to boil on the family's new electric stove. Maman made bread last night and it still has the fresh-baked smell. Beth toasts two pieces of the fragrant loaf in a skillet. She leaves the toast on the wood table in the living room. She sets out butter and pear jam in case Maman comes out of her bedroom later.

They made the jam together last fall when the pear trees dropped hundreds of sweet fruit all at once. The trees had been here for many generations. Last fall, Maman was up and about and decided that something had to be done with all the pears. They boiled down huge pans of them with loads of sugar and then poured the jam into glass jars to gel. The batch lasted all year.

Listening to the teapot whine, whistle, and scream, it occurs to Beth that if she walks the two miles to school without stopping, then she will only miss her science class. She could make it to art class, second period. Art is her favorite class.

Beth pours the water over chamomile flowers to make tea. She collected the flowers from the backyard beside the house. The thyme and mint and lemon balm, her family had planted those, but the chamomile grows everywhere as a wildflower. She turns off the stove. The little flower with the mounded yellow center surrounded by a row of feathery white petals always reminds her of women's eyes and eyelashes. Sometimes she draws pictures of them that way. In moonlight, the chamomile blossoms glow when they are alive and connected to the plant that nourishes them. Right now, steeping in the boiling water, they are wet and they look like they are crying. The musty scent of chamomile fills the room.

She hears Maman singing softly in the adjacent bedroom. The song is unfamiliar to her, something about columbine flowers sleeping in the forest and waiting for her love to come. Beth is curious about whom Maman's love might be for a moment; it's certainly not Da. She thinks it's better to focus on the flowers, because some things about Maman are better off left as a mystery.

Columbine wildflowers have a haunting, abnormal beauty and Beth treasures them. She's read that they have magical properties, at least to witches who know how to unlock their secrets.

Beth doesn't know any witches.

To her, the pink-red columbine buds before they open look like a human heart suspended from a delicate stem. She's drawn them like that. But after the blossoms burst open, each flower resembles a group of five, blood-red doves clustered together in a miniature dance. She thinks the flowers are waiting to fly.

The sound of Maman singing means it's fine for Beth to go to school. Even if it is a sad song, the act of singing means things will be better later. Maman will be alright today. Beth checks that the printer has paper in it and that Maman's cell phone is charged, the volume is on. If she wants to start writing, everything is ready for her here.

Beth packs up her bookbag and slips on sneakers. She collects the charcoal drawings that she made over the last few months for the final art class project. She nestles the drawings in a zippered portfolio. She usually draws with charcoal, so most of her work is in black and white. Sometimes she uses colored paper, and once in a while she works with colored Conté crayons for red, or chalk for blue or green. Certain colors mean a lot to her. Like the special hazel that is the color of Maman's eyes, that's a good color.

Beth heads out, walking to school with her bookbag on her back and the art portfolio over her shoulder. The plant parts of her drawings are good—she's certain of that. But what will the teacher's reaction be to the drawings of plant-human-animal combinations she's created as chimeras? She's not sure at all.

10 AM

Beth's eighth-grade science teacher sees her as he closes the door of the empty classroom behind him. "Are you alright?" he stops her.

After her long trek from home, she's sweating but not out of breath. "I'm really sorry I missed your class, Mr. Heller," she says.

"No. No, don't be sorry. I mean, you're not hurt?"

Beth frowns at him and shakes her head, no. Mr. Heller is always a bit odd. She suspects that he is what doctors call *paranoid*, one of the new words she learned from the school psychologist she meets with every week. If Mr. Heller's not paranoid, at the very least he has an unusually high level of anxiety.

He says, "You weren't on the bus."

"No." She pushes a damp tendril of hair back from her face. She watches the school psychologist enter the classroom across the hall, then looks back at Mr. Heller.

He grimaces and shrugs. He reaches into his bag, pulls out his planner, and gives her a handout sheet. "Here, take it. You can work on it later. You have Internet access at home?"

She nods.

"Good, that's all you'll need. Go through this by tomorrow. And would you please come to class? We're having a discussion. You're a catalyst, Beth. I want you in the room."

She takes the paper and hurries over to her art class. *Catalyst.* That's new. She doesn't know the word. Not catlike, probably; she expects it has something to do with science.

Beth walks into art class on time. She sees the psychologist sitting with one of the students, a tall, thin girl who is sobbing, trying to catch her breath. The student sputters but can't speak. Beth is unable to make out what the student is trying to say, something about death. Half the desks are empty, and half the students who came look damaged. Beth thinks they may have been in a fight. This must have been an unusually big fight.

She slowly lowers herself into the seat at her desk and takes out her folder of drawings from her portfolio. The art teacher walks through the room, stopping at each desk to collect all the student projects one by one.

"*Chimera Me.*" The teacher reads Beth's project title, picking up the folder. She smiles quickly at Beth, then walks to the front of the room with the stack of student artwork. The teacher sits down at her desk and sorts the folders.

Beth is surprised to feel like a part of her is missing now that the drawings she had been working on for so long are suddenly gone. She leans the empty portfolio against her knees under the desk.

A police officer opens the classroom door.

"Officer Joe," the art teacher says and she stands up. She doesn't even reach the top of his shoulders. "You need a few minutes with the class?"

"You can stay, Muriel," Officer Joe says, and he moves to the front of the classroom.

"I know that what happened this morning was tough. Some of us feel angry about the accident. I'm sorry about your friends who got hurt. I spoke with the med techs. The other kids on the bus will be alright, all of them. I want you to know that. They got a few stitches, nothing that won't heal."

The girl at the back of the room immediately stops crying.

He continues. "Now this is important. And I want you to listen. Don't go down to the gas drilling site. It's off limits. Don't go down there at all, not for any reason. Don't drive down there, don't walk there either. I've come by and said this before, and I'll probably have to say it again. Where they're drilling isn't a place to play. Not a place to hang out, not even to walk around in anymore. So whatever you may feel like doing, if it's at the drilling site, you can't do it. Stay away from there.

"One other thing. You leave the people over there working for the energy company alone. The one truck driver, yes, he made a mistake. We're talking to him down at the police station. He's one individual; his problem doesn't have to be everyone else's. Don't make it yours."

He turns to the art teacher, "Muriel, that's all I have."

Muriel raises her eyebrows, watching him leave. She turns back to the silent faces of her students. They are each contorted in a different way with private pain she feels certain she won't understand. She wonders where to begin and decides that she'll have them draw to let out what they are feeling. She hands out blank paper along with red and black Conté crayon sticks.

Officer Joe addresses the students in each classroom, the same speech over and over.

He meets with the school principal, who doesn't have much to say that interests him. Mostly, the principal wants Joe to do something about the twins who are supposed to graduate this year, Mark and Matt. The principal doesn't like the twins. Joe already knows that; the principal never did like them. They're strong and strong-minded too. Now, daily, the principal has become more and more convinced that the twins are a bad influence on the younger, junior high students. The principal is somewhat afraid of the boys on a personal level, although he can't put a finger on why that is. He wants Joe to be the one to get them out.

Joe has his own reasons for not wanting to disrupt Mark and Matt's education. He promised their mother, a friend of his, that he'd keep an eye on them, before she shipped out to Afghanistan. He doesn't think that means letting them drop out of high school. She didn't come back from her last deployment. Joe's been stopping in to check on her sons once or twice every week at the home she left behind. Joe is a man of his word.

When he stops by the school nurse's small office, she has a lot to say. She reminds him that she knows each of the children she had to patch up and comfort this morning, and she knows most of their families. He does too. She goes on and on about the truck driver, about the trucks in general, how many trips they make up and down her once quiet street. She blames them for the destruction of her peace of mind. She wants to know what Joe will be doing about all of it.

Joe knows she's right to be outraged by the truck accident, and he agrees with her on more than one of her points. He should be doing something, he thinks. He's not sure what.

11 AM

Waiting at the local health clinic, Charlotte Smith reads the signs on the walls over and over to pass the time. She hates going to the doctor. She wishes she didn't have to come here alone. Bringing her husband David is out of the question. Some things can't be shared with him, and the visit to the clinic is one of them. He wouldn't understand the condition she's in now. Her daughter Beth might have come, but Charlotte doesn't want to trouble her.

The clinic signs are printed on a swirly pale blue and light gray background. They detail what to do when you are expecting a baby. Free medical care, counseling, and adoption services are described with arrows pointing to Websites and phone numbers.

"You are not alone," they all seem to say, in soft, caring tones.

She marvels at how things have changed from the time when she had Beth. Then, teen pregnancy was a secret. Her family found out eventually, of course. They were disgraced. When they realized she would never give up the baby, her parents left Charlotte here with the baby's father, David. The rest of her family moved back to the old place in New Orleans with their aunts, uncles, and cousins. They left the land to Charlotte, to help her with her future in a way they couldn't by staying with her. The shame was too much for them.

Charlotte never understood the concept of shame; everything had a place, a time in her world, following the rules of nature.

The process has changed now at the medical clinic, she thinks, even if not in families. The circumstances, and possibilities that remain open, these all shape the outcomes of a pregnancy as a blessing or a tragedy. Charlotte is of the opinion that any child is a blessing, but she knows from experience that some people do not agree, people like her own family.

A nurse walks into the waiting room. "Charlotte Smith?" The nurse seems happy to see her.

Charlotte follows her into an examination room. She slips off her shoes and steps on the scale.

"You stopped losing weight. Wonderful," the nurse says. "One hundred twenty pounds—good. The same as last week. Feeling better?"

"Ah, no. I'm still so tired. It's horrible, really. I have to sleep in the afternoon. And I get the migraines." The words tumble out even though Charlotte has the impression that the nurse isn't much interested.

"What are you doing for your headaches?"

"Sleeping. Keeping the room dark."

The nurse smiles at her. "I'll bring it up with the doctor. You're eating?"

Charlotte nods as the nurse takes her blood pressure.

"Normal. The doctor will be right in, maybe five minutes," the nurse says and she leaves the room.

Waiting for the doctor to come by, alone in the air-conditioned room, Charlotte feels cold. She stares at the blank, blue computer screen. She thinks of Sara, who dropped her off this morning, and the disturbing things she shared. The latest story was about what the doctor told Sara not long ago. Sara and her husband were trying to have a family. They had been trying for three years, but with no luck at all. Now, no child was in Sara's future. What was life for them without children? For Sara, it was an emptiness, a failure.

Poisoned, Sara had said.

Ruined, Charlotte had thought.

*****

Dr. Miller walks in and races through her records on the computer screen. Patient: Charlotte Smith, age twenty-eight. The doctor checks the last visit's lab results. Blood work shows anemia, but no HBV, HCV, HIV. Luckily, this patient is virus free.

The doctor has fewer than seven minutes for the visit. She'll see a minimum of eight and up to ten patients every hour today and has a lot to accomplish for each one of them.

She prepares the tubes for blood work in a rack set up on the counter near the door. Preventive care screening should include a number of things she knows she won't have time for, and so she picks what she feels are likely to be the most relevant ones. Abuse and alcoholism, these are things the rural areas like Brindle have a lot of, she thinks.

"How are you feeling? How are things at home?" Dr. Miller asks.

Charlotte smiles, but she doesn't know what to say.

"Do you feel safe there?"

Charlotte frowns. What a question. Dr. Miller always asks these kinds of questions. Safe. Does she feel safe anywhere? *What is safe?*

"Things are the same at home. But my husband has less work now. He builds, you know. And before, he was always so busy. No one builds here now. I'm worried about him. Safe, I don't know..."

"You aren't afraid at home?" Dr. Miller looks over at Charlotte. "He doesn't hurt you?"

Charlotte grimaces. "No, no, he is a good man. But if I could ask something—not about me, not about home. I wanted to ask you about this. My friend who drove me today, when she came by two days ago she told me that something very strange is going on here, where we live, here in Brindle."

Dr. Miller listens, unwrapping the needle and syringe packets.

Charlotte whispers, "She thinks we've been poisoned."

Dr. Miller raises her eyebrows as she slips a needle into Charlotte's arm for the blood test.

"My friend Sara had a urine test. *Phenol*, they told her."

The doctor jerks her head back. "Phenol!"

Charlotte nods. She remembers how Sara looked. "Spots on her skin were bleeding. Oozing. Seeing her like that, it scared me."

"Bleeding where?" Dr. Miller watches the blood fill the syringe through the narrow plastic tubing. The color is not the deep red it should be, but paler.

"On her face and her hands," Charlotte says. "In spots, not all over. *Phenol*, they told her, you know?"

"Don't move, one moment. We're almost finished. Naturally that would be upsetting to you, or to anyone, for that matter. I understand. That's terrible!"

Dr. Miller runs through the facts about phenol she can recall. She worked with phenol as a college student in the lab for biochemistry research. Phenol dissolved and destroyed proteins. It was used to clean protein off when purifying DNA and other molecules from living cells. Gloves and good ventilation were mandatory. They kept the DNA for experiments, and then the phenol waste was disposed of as a biohazard. She wonders where that went. She never thought about it before, where biohazard wastes went, other than in the red containers in the corners of the lab. Maybe they were taken to a place like Brindle, or to Brindle itself, somewhere in a hazardous-waste disposal site.

"Where does your friend work?" the doctor asks.

"Ah, she doesn't. We were out berry picking. Strawberries are in season, you know. I picked twenty-five quarts and she picked thirty. We always put up jam in the summers here. Anyway, it was after that. I thought you might know about this, the phenol."

Dr. Miller leaves the needle and tubing in Charlotte's arm and connects another syringe to collect more blood. Her patient is very pale but the tips of her fingers are stained pink, possibly from the berries. The doctor thinks she'll run a few more tests. She remembers that people still hunt and gather here, primitive habits that didn't change with the times.

"Phenol—that's an industrial chemical. I wouldn't expect to find it in the urine. It's a poison. There." The doctor removes the needle and presses on Charlotte's skin with folded sterile gauze where a drop of blood forms. "We're finished. Press on this, please. Let's get a urine sample today before you leave."

Charlotte holds the gauze down on her skin.

Dr. Miller knows that phenol enters the body a number of ways. It can get into the lungs by inhalation. It can be eaten in contaminated foods. Phenol gets in through the eyes from the air, or the skin by direct contact. Once inside the body, phenol damages the organs, the liver and the kidneys. You can't live without the organs. As little as a gram of phenol is lethal and kills a person by respiratory failure. The body can't breathe.

Smaller amounts of phenol cause stomach problems over time, damage the central nervous system, the brain and spine, cause cancer. In some cases, phenol makes skin lesions that may bleed.

The doctor understands that phenol is caustic. From experience, she knows it burns. A graduate student in the lab that Dr. Miller trained in had a phenol spill. The student kept her phenol on an upper shelf at her section of the lab bench, a terrible idea. For safety, you were supposed to keep phenol bottles at bench level to avoid spills. When the student reached for it and the bottle fell, the colorless, thick substance ran down her arm and over the left side of her face.

She had been a pretty student, beautiful really, before the accident. Afterwards, she was scarred for life. Bright red, the scar was terrible. It was hideous.

Dr. Miller reminds herself to look up phenol's effects and the potential treatments; in case another incident comes in, one like this patient's friend. She is surprised that none of the staff mentioned the phenol case to her. If the phenol exposure is from the environment, then if one person was contaminated, surely there will be more. Industrial toxins and poisons are in the air, in the water, even in the local food in certain places. Brindle, though remote, is no exception. Here, it is the chemicals associated with gas drilling, hydraulic fracturing, that are a concern in their area.

The State Medical Society looked at all the evidence; she read the report. Their advice was to ban fracking. The Society called for a moratorium, a halt to gas drilling. The ban was to prevent damage to people's health and devastating effects on the rest of the environment, the animals and plants. Dr. Miller remembers that many chemicals, over six hundred, are either used in the process of the drilling or are found in the hazardous waste. Both, possibly.

She thinks that contamination from the drilling is a possibility here.

Charlotte watches a wet circle spread on the cotton fibers of the gauze. The color is pale red. "Is this how it's supposed to look?" she asks.

"You're anemic, but we'll do the blood count. I'll run a few tests. You're going to need vitamins, maybe an injection. What have you been eating?" The doctor finishes with the tubes. She labels each of them while Charlotte lists the normal things in her daily diet.

"Strawberries, of course. Almonds. I bake bread..."

"No meat?"

Charlotte shakes her head.

"Why not?" Dr. Miller asks.

"Because of the goat."

"What goat?"

"The first people I worked for had a pet goat, for cheese, you know. They made their own cheese. They ran a resort, the one on the hill. Anderson's. You know it?"

"Anderson's...no."

"I loved that goat, fed it for them, you know. They killed it in the fall. The owner, Mrs. Anderson, baked the skull with the brains in it. She made me eat the brains. I probably ate more tears than brains, but I had to. She made me. I was young. I had to work. You know how it is. Supposed to be a delicacy. Can you imagine? They eat their goat's brains."

Never ask a patient a question you don't want to hear the answer to, Dr. Miller reminds herself. "How old were you?"

"That was the year I had Beth, so I was fifteen. I don't eat meat," Charlotte says simply.

"You're going to need a source of protein and iron," Dr. Miller says.

She always feels uncomfortable during Charlotte Smith's visits. The patient is unusual. It could be from exposure to toxins, or it might be a mood disorder. The doctor worries about the possibility of depression. Then again, exposure to the chemical toluene has been reported in the area in the past three months. One of the cases was right here in this clinic, a male high school student.

Dr. Miller remembers that at first, when the boy was brought to the clinic unconscious, the staff suspected drug overdose. He had never been to the clinic before. From what records the staff could locate by calling the nearest hospitals, he had not seen a doctor since his childhood vaccinations. The case turned out to be toluene poisoning when the blood work came back, and Dr. Miler still believed it was from sniffing some kind of solvent to get high.

Luckily the patient lived, although high levels of inhaled toluene can be fatal—respiratory failure. When

Dr. Miller did a family history, she found that the patient had a twin. They had a suicide in the family. Their mother was single, a soldier. She killed herself while she was in the service. More soldiers have died from suicide than combat these last few years, most often by opioid pain medication overdose—that was the case here.

Dr. Miller did the suicide screening questionnaire with the boy when he came around. He seemed psychologically healthy to her and they sent him home with his twin brother.

Later, they learned that certain places in the area around Brindle were, in fact, contaminated with industrial toluene. It worries her that chemical toluene causes some of the symptoms her patient Charlotte shows: fatigue, headache, and depression. Like phenol, toluene is also a carcinogen. Most concerning to Dr. Miller is the effect of toxic toluene on fetal development in pregnant women. Babies can be born underweight or have delayed bone formation. Toluene can cause abnormal growth of the arms, legs, and head. She's not sure how to bring it up. She checks the time and decides that she'll stick to the usual preventive screens for today.

She faces Charlotte. "And how often did you drink, say, in the past week?" She asks.

"I'm not drinking."

"Good."

"Except for when I met up with my friend Henry from the city. He visits sometimes."

"When was that?"

"A few days ago," Charlotte says.

The doctor looks at her and enters something into the records. "And when your friend came to visit, your friend Sara?"

Charlotte nods.

"And that was this week too." Dr. Miller isn't sure about how alcohol might interact with phenol or toluene, if her patient has also been exposed. The patient has too many risk factors. The doctor feels more and more alarmed.

Charlotte shrugs. "I've stopped, for the most part, you know. But the headaches, they're still terrible for me."

"I can give you something for that. Have you talked things over with your husband yet?"

"No."

"I know we spoke about it at your last visit. Are you sure this is what you both want?"

"It's three months now. And I'm a Catholic," Charlotte says, as if this explains everything. She wonders why people talk about "what you want," as if it is a choice.

"Yes, I remember now. I'm sorry." Dr. Miller closes her eyes. She begins again. "How is your daughter doing at school?"

"Beth is fine. Beth is an angel, a gift from God."

"Great." Dr. Miller has run out of time, but she must try to accomplish one more thing here. "I'm concerned about...let me ask...you're not using the tap water for anything, are you? You're using the bottled water?"

"Yes, yes, of course I use the special water. They still bring us water every week. They bring my friend Sara and her husband water too. They can't use their water. The well at their place exploded two weeks ago, you know. It's still burning."

Dr. Miller draws in a deep breath. "Sara's certainly having a really bad time of it. Mrs. Smith, is it possible...could you move...is there somewhere else you can go? For a few months even, until the baby comes? I'd like you to think about it. Please. You've stopped losing weight, but you're not gaining yet either. You should be, by now. I think you know that."

Dr. Miller is frustrated when her patient gives her a blank look. This is the look that means they don't understand each other. She must say something explicit about the risks. She has to get through to her.

"We have to think about your health, and the baby's, too. I can't say much about it, but the environment, Mrs. Smith, the environment here, it's not healthy for you. Chemicals here in the ground, in the water, they could harm an unborn child—your unborn child. In fact, they would, they will. That's not even really in question."

So many things come to mind that Dr. Miller would like to tell her. She shouldn't. She can't even, unless they are directly related to her care.

Following inquiries to the energy company about chemical contamination, the medical staff is restricted to giving information only on a need-to-know basis. The gag order here chokes her. It chokes all of them. She finds it insufferable. In some areas doctors have sued to regain the right of free speech and their obligation to report local public health hazards. Whenever she sees "nondisclosure", "confidentiality", or "proprietary compounds", what comes to her mind next is that somewhere, someone is about to lie, cheat, or steal. She expects that they probably already have.

Dr. Miller wants to tell her patient that toxins travel from the environment to the mother and then to the baby. Not only alcohol, but poisons like the chemical toluene are shared with the unborn baby through the mother's blood and body fluids. Worse, the radioactive materials in the industrial wastes deposited by the gas drilling sites in the evaporation pits; these also travel from mother to child. She wants to say that hundreds of chemicals contaminate the blood of newborn babies here, linked to everything from organ damage to disability and mental illness. Toxins show up in the amniotic fluid that the fetus floats in, and then later, in the mother's milk.

There must be a place that is safer to have the baby than Brindle.

Charlotte looks down at her hands in her lap. She sighs deeply. "Do you mean like what happened to the fish? When all the fish died here, the fish and the salamanders?"

Dr. Miller nods. "It could be. When was that, exactly?"

"Three months ago."

"The same time as—"

"—Yes, please don't say it. Did you know my little cat died last week?"

"I'm sorry."

"We are poisoned here."

"I think this is a real possibility, unfortunately," Dr. Miller says.

"I have family in Louisiana, in New Orleans. And in France, in Marseille. I have family there too. They live in the city," Charlotte says.

She tears up. "I don't like the city, you know. I really don't like it, not at all."

Dr. Miller smiles at her and takes her hand. "See if you can visit, won't you? I'm not sure what your place is like in New Orleans after the flood, but in France the environment is cleaner. They banned fracking there."

Charlotte looks up at her. "I know. I saw that in the news."

"Please," the doctor says. "Try. Do it for the baby. Do it for her future."

Noon

Brindle Central School closes early, after the accident with the hazardous waste truck and the school bus at Smith's Lane. The principal and staff call parents. Beth waits in the midday heat with hundreds of students gathered in front of the school building. Today they are unusually quiet.

When she gets into Da's truck, it smells faintly of chocolate and strongly of fresh greens. Beth turns to the back to see what Da brought with him. It looks like he was on his way home from the store when the school called. She hasn't eaten all day. She hopes he got things Maman will cook, and she expects that he did.

They drive home in silence. Anything remotely touching on the gas drilling in Brindle is likely to set Da off. He hates the drilling. Although Beth wishes she could talk to him about the accident, she knows she can't. Him exploding within the confines of a vehicle is unthinkable. Maman says his temper is because of what happened to him when he was away in the service. He never talks about it.

Beth wants to tell him what everyone at school is saying: A trucker got high this morning before he headed out to the gas drilling site. He accidentally ran his tanker into the school bus crossing over Route 32 onto their road. Twelve of the children went to the clinic and then home for the day. Twenty-three more are shook up, but not hurt. The bus driver, old Nan DesChamps, is dead. She had a heart attack.

Beth imagines that Da already heard all of this when the school called him. She expects that he is probably trying as hard as she is to not talk about the accident at this very moment.

She takes out the papers that the science teacher, Mr. Heller, gave her earlier in the morning, nine terms in alphabetical order. She reads to herself: *arsenic, benzene, carcinogen, ethyl benzene, heavy metal, mercury, methane, radioactivity, selenium.* Part 1: Define each term in your own words answering these four questions: What is it? Where does it come from and where does it go? How does it affect living things? Why should you know about it? Part 2: Highlight each of the new words in news articles. The news is copied in at the bottom of the sheet and goes on to the next page.

Beth smiles. Defining *arsenic* is easy—that's a poison. She imagines nearly everyone knows about arsenic because of the old movie *Arsenic and Old Lace*. She isn't sure where arsenic comes from or ends up, but it definitely kills people. You should know about it so it doesn't kill you.

Heavy metal is a music style, her least favorite. It makes her want to mute the volume, leave the room, or anything just to get away from it. She suspects that *heavy metal* is probably also some kind of chemical.

Mercury is a small planet, a god with wings on his feet. No idea where *mercury* comes from or goes.

Radioactivity—easy—comes from other planets, according to comics and maybe in real life. Comets or asteroids or something like that. The others she will have to search when she gets home. She thinks she will probably search them all.

Beth reaches out and puts her hand gently on her father's shoulder. He doesn't look over at her. "Thanks for driving me, Da." She sees his ears move up slightly and the skin around his eyes crinkle, like it does when he tries not to smile.

When they get home, Da carries the groceries into the kitchen. Beth helps him put the things away in silence. Maman isn't home. Neither of them knows where she is. Lunch will have to wait.

Da goes to his study to read, and Beth goes out to the barn to feeds the horse, Jolie. Beth listens to the horse eating for a few minutes, then leaves her and wanders out to the pond behind the barn.

The pond is about a quarter of an acre in all, separated from the neighbor's swamp by a narrow strip of land. The water is alive, filled with fascinating creatures. Some of the residents are a quick rainbow of colors, like the iridescent bluegill fish with their graceful fins waving like little hands. She sometimes draws them like that, with hands. Others, like the gray bullfrogs, are dull and prehistoric looking. A bloom of algae is growing on the sunny side of the pond, bubbling up in translucent green orbs. She imagines that the bubbles are filled with newly generated oxygen from photosynthesis here in the full sun. Cattails grow up from the water along one side. Red-winged blackbirds nest in the tall reeds; they do every year.

Beth loves to watch the community of living creatures in their pond. She has ever since she could walk out here. Da used to say that she was going to be a biologist, when Beth was younger. She laughs, remembering that she didn't know what the word meant. *Biologist.* She thought it sounded like a disease.

The pond water is cloudy today. In the full sun, shadows of turtles, fish, and snakes are visible. She counts five big snakes hugging the north side of the pond, moving slowly around one another and through the water plants in tight circles. They are black, as thick as Beth's wrist and longer than she is tall.

Sometimes Da shoots at the snakes. Beth thinks that bullets don't travel under water well. If they did, the snakes would be dead.

The things Beth can see are less frightening than the things she can't, like the snapping turtle Da says lives in the mud at the bottom of the pond. The turtle sleeps all winter and wakes up at each spring thaw. Beth knows this, because the baby ducklings swimming behind the mother mallard duck disappear one by one. They are pulled from the surface down below, right as she watches. They are there, and then there is a little rippling circle where they were, and they are gone. This makes the mallard frantic. She flaps insanely and calls out, quacking hysterically. Beth thinks it must be terrible to lose the baby and not know where it has gone. The ducklings disappear, just like that. Every year, the mallard hatches a new brood anyway. Beth isn't sure if she is stupid or endlessly optimistic, continuing this cycle year after year. But like Beth, the mallard can't see the snapping turtle; she only knows her chicks disappear behind her.

Snapping turtles can get to be very large. Beth isn't sure how large. She thinks that her bare toes under water might look a lot like the sort of small fish snapping turtles like to eat. Wading in the water here is out of the question. Fast-moving water like the stream that runs through the forest is fine for wading, but not the pond. She has too much work to do, the final science project and the history paper, and can't go down to the stream now, but maybe later. Yes—that will be her reward.

A ripple, and then following it, a gray mound pushes through the water near the pond's bank. The nose, head, and then the body and shell of an old snapping turtle emerge slowly from the pond. He crawls steadily, dragging himself up onto the strip of land beside the pond. He stops there, opposite Beth.

She's never seen anything move so slowly. He completely blocks the path, as large as half the kitchen table top. Grand and primitive, he holds his head up like a dinosaur. He is a great, great-grandfather turtle. She imagines that he is surprised to see the changes on the surface of the earth after what must have been a hundred years under the mud in the bottom of their pond. She wonders whether he's ever seen their barn before today.

He moves his narrow gray head ever so slowly on a long, leathery brownish neck extended from his huge shell. His mouth is more like a beak, a tremendous and mechanical-looking hook.

A shot rings out. The old snapping turtle jolts. He bleeds lavender-pink blood from his neck in a smooth, slow stream. The blood pools, a thick and medicinal bluish-pink, a strange, sad, sickening color. The ancient head slowly lowers to the ground.

Beth backs away silently and leans against the barn, watching the turtle die. She looks back at the house and sees Da's silhouette visible through the open window.

1 PM

Officer Joe has it stuck in his mind that he should pay another visit to the eighth-grade art teacher, Muriel, after the students have all left school for the day. They were dismissed early on account of the accident, and so he thinks she may be alone.

He finds her sitting and organizing papers in the classroom. Her desk is flooded with angry, messy drawings in black and red, of buses, children, ambulances, and trucks. Joe pauses beside Muriel and looks over the drawings. One stands out from the rest, a field of red columbine flowers growing up out of black ashes. A picture without a name. He finds it fascinating.

"Good for them, drawing, isn't it?" he asks and she nods. Joe goes on, "Shows their feelings."

Muriel says, "They express themselves. A small thing, really, but maybe it helps somehow. I believe it can. Art therapy. Some people recommend it."

"Say, Muriel, have you ever seen anything like these?" Joe shows her a photo he took and saved on his cell phone. A tall storage tower on a hill is covered in artistic graffiti. Plant forms overlap with human body parts. Roses and rose petals beside tongues; chamomile plants with human eyes as flowers; human fingers curling out from unfolding fern fronds.

Muriel is an artist herself with her own studio. She even gives art classes on the side. He thinks that if anyone might have a clue about who the vandal is, Muriel would.

She looks at the phone and then quickly pulls away from Joe.

He says, "I took these yesterday. Here, here's more." He shows her another photo of a defaced water truck, spray-painted with a fly bearing a horse head. He watches her reaction. She seems conflicted to him, interested and repulsed at the same time.

"These belong to someone you know?" Joe asks.

She nods. "Maybe."

"Who is it, Muriel?"

"Do I have to say?"

"No. But if you do, I can let him know about the problem he's getting himself into. You know where I took this one?" He shows her another photo, a scrawled painting of a human arm emerging like a tumor from the side of a fish.

Muriel takes a deep breath and holds it, counting to ten inside. She says, "I don't, no."

"At one of the gas wells, that's where. Here's another one, at one of the storage sites."

"Storing what?" she asks.

"Toxic chemicals."

She rolls her eyes and shakes her head.

"You get my point," he says.

"The Smith girl, Joe. That's her style."

"No. David and Charlotte's daughter? Beth Smith?" Joe asks.

"Quite the talented young lady," Muriel says.

Joe puts away his phone slowly. He does not look forward to talking with his friend David about this.

"And a fool like her mother, looks like," Muriel continues.

"Don't be mean," Joe says. "No need for that. Can't blame the parents for what the kids do. Maybe she inherited the creativity—that's a good thing. You have any of Beth's other artwork here? I'd like to take a look if you do."

Muriel still has the end-of-the-year art projects out on her desk. She has no way to hide Beth's project, but she wishes she did. She sits down and pushes the folder of drawings over toward him. "These are hers."

"*Chimera Me*." He reads the title and slowly opens the folder. He wonders whether Beth will be an artist. He thinks of the leogryph chimera—lion's body, eagle's wings, parrot's beak. He saw it carved with a beautiful woman rider in one of the treasures found at Bagram, not far from Kabul, Afghanistan, where he was stationed. For some reason, the carving reminded him of David's Beth.

The drawings inside the folder are combinations of plants, animals, and human body parts joined together in bizarre chimeras, but not like the leogryph. This collection of originals looks even more realistic and freakish than what he saw scrawled on the trucks at the drilling site. These look more like mutants than mythological animal creatures. They are delicately sketched and shaded and have more detail than the graffiti.

He shudders. The drawings trigger Joe's memories of carnage from war zones along the oil pipeline he patrolled with his squad in Afghanistan. Those sights are permanently etched in his mind. The images come to life in his nightmares. He tries to wipe the thought from his mind and press forward.

"Looks pretty much the same, doesn't it?" he asks, not expecting an answer.

"You don't need to keep them, do you, Joe?"

He carefully closes the folder and hands it to Muriel. "They're not mine. I'll go have a visit with her family. We can't have kids going down there," he says.

No, we can't, Muriel thinks and she watches him walk away.

Officer Joe was in the National Guard before the police force. Muriel knows he's seen some things. He's done some things too, she imagines. Although she's grateful that he's looking out for the best interests of the students, at the same time she is wary of Joe. Truthfully, she's afraid of him. Most of the people in the community here are too. She keeps a distance from Joe. It's not because he is a man with a gun; everyone here has a gun at home. No, she is more afraid of Joe than other men because he has a gun and he would not hesitate to use it on a person, if he thought that he should.

Muriel wishes she knew of a way to stop the kids from trespassing. She's angry that their parents don't have better control over them. She opens Beth's art project folder and meditates on the opening drawing. A ghostly human heart is suspended from a thin plant stem beside a red columbine flower bud. Beside it, blood-red doves hover.

2 PM

Henry Berger planned to inspect the soil and water on a private property today, on account of a report about a dead cat. The place is five miles from a main gas drilling site and about two miles from the public school. The owner filed the complaint shortly after a wastewater leak was reported from fracking at a horizontal well. It ran under their place.

Henry pulls himself together after the school bus accident. At the police station, he and Adrian stop by and describe what they saw, how the truck slammed into the bus and then pulled off the road. The police assure them that the trucker is in custody and that all the kids are going to be just fine. Intending to start his day over, Henry heads out to the inspection site with Adrian.

These kinds of problems, the ones Henry is brought in to work on for the energy company, like reports of dead pets, are not the kinds of problems he experiences where he lives in the city. Not to say that as a homeowner in Brooklyn he has no problems, or that his pets have never died there. But he doesn't worry about a pet dying from the water supply. New York City water, *it's reliable*. This is one of the things people say that actually do make sense to him.

In Brooklyn, Henry has other kinds of problems. The day he left to come up here, for example, he noticed a man he didn't recognize on the street in front of the house. At first, Henry thought the man looked like everyone else: shaved head, big gut, brown shirt, gray jeans. That was until he saw the handcuffs on the man's belt. Then he noticed the sunglasses and the gun hanging at the man's side.

Looking closer, Henry saw two older men he did recognize who lived on the block. They were crouching, pushed unnaturally up against a car. The car was already stripped bare by a man wearing dark blue, who was pulling out everything he could, looking for something. Then it seemed like he found it. One of the older men smiled drunkenly, red-faced and embarrassed. Henry thought that night would be a hell of a sobering for the poor guy. The other older man was shorter and very thin. He struggled against a restraint on his wrists.

Henry watched the scene from the concrete steps leading up to his place. He didn't speak to anyone about it. Neighbors watched silently from their steps and from open windows. Although they had an unspoken rule of not looking at other people's business, everyone stared without apology. No, the new man was not like everyone else, not at all. He was not one of the local men, he was a narc.

One of the reasons Henry wanted to bring Adrian to Brindle is because here he doesn't have to worry about the drug trade. He also won't have to be anxious about Adrian being stopped and searched by the police, which happens all the time to young men who live in Brooklyn.

Today Henry's work trip should be better than usual, because he has Adrian along with him for the ride. They pull up at the side of the road and Henry turns off the car. He looks at his son, how he leans forward in the seat and smiles. Henry expects that Adrian's happy; he seems interested in this new world.

"Let's see what they've got," Henry says.

Henry speaks the same language as the people who live in Brindle, English. Yet in a way, he doesn't. The things people say out here, and say over and over, are not the same things he says. Certainly they are not the same things he thinks.

His science background is one thing he doesn't share with most of the local residents. He's afraid that his interests and experiences don't overlap much at all with theirs either. Even more important, he suspects that his values are different. He thinks of himself as a man of science and a liberal. The people he's met here are so conservative that they're practically Libertarian. He thinks maybe they are in fact Libertarian, but he doesn't ask. Big on individual freedoms, he also finds that people here are hard-nosed about the letter of the law.

Take the incident last week, for example. A local woman was arrested and taken to jail for trespassing on the energy company property where they were drilling for gas, property she used to own. When she got out, she sued them, charging that the energy company was trespassing on her body by contaminating the water she drank. *Right back at you,* the news headline read. He finds it baffling the way people out here think about things.

Henry dislikes going onto other people's private property like he has to today. They all own guns, for one thing. Some people even display them in the house. Henry is an anxious person by nature and he suffers from panic attacks, so the idea of guns in the house scares him. To make things worse, most people here don't seem to have a positive opinion about him, not when he first arrives. This makes him feel even more nervous about the guns. Some people are interested in his work after a while, but only a small minority. He has a whole host of complicated reasons he'd rather be in the lab or an office than the field.

Several of the houses out here were listed as saturated—and some supersaturated—with methane, a flammable gas. Henry thinks that this house may very well be one of them. He bought an electric car because the idea of riding in a car with a combustion engine in areas that might be full of an explosive gas like methane freaked him out completely. Henry is not a risk taker. He brings a backpack with his tools for sampling water and dirt, his laptop, and his cell phone.

The place is a wood-frame farmhouse set back from the road by half an acre of lawn dotted with wildflowers. A great oak stands in the front yard. He thinks the tree must be over a hundred years old, by the size of it. Behind the house he sees a small barn. The owners, the Smiths—whom Smith's Lane is named for—are the only remaining family in this area who have neither sold nor leased their land for gas drilling.

The Smith property comes to only four acres. Henry imagines they'll give it up soon. The arguments to be made for relocating are compelling. Even when people resist, they can be forced to give up the land in one way or another, through eminent domain if necessary in the end. The government has been squarely on the side of the energy companies in most of these cases and has obliged by seizing land. The act is justified by the need for economic development. The new business is in the public interest, the dominant theory goes.

So much for land ownership, Henry thinks; it's a modern myth. You can buy and sell rights to use the land; you can't actually own it. He tries to remember who said, *the land doesn't belong to you, you belong to the land*; the author was certainly Native American, but he can't pin down the source.

Henry researched the company maps before he came and knows that the place has its own artesian well. Having one of these was thought of as an asset in the past. Many of the places here have a well on their property. No water is piped in to these remote areas, so wells are necessary. He also knows that farther back on the property is a pond, and behind it, a stream flowing from a natural spring. He will need a sample from all of these sources of water, and probably the dirt as well.

Henry knocks at the door. A sharp whack and the snap of breaking wood resonate from behind the house. Henry jumps.

Adrian nudges his father, and then he walks around the house to check out the noise. Out back, Adrian sees a man about the same age as his father, but taller and twice as big around. He is built like a superhero from a comic book. The imposing man swings a huge ax and splits a log in two with a loud crack. Hundreds of split wood pieces are stacked neatly against the house.

Listening to the rhythm of the work, Adrian thinks about starting a new song. *Breaking wood, killing time, breaking a box, making mine*...Adrian leans against the house and watches, humming softly. "Hmm, hmm, killing time..."

Henry stands and waits at the front of the house in the midday heat. He wonders what he'll find in the water here at the Smith place. Water that comes from deep beneath the earth is not necessarily better than water running in the streams; that's a common misconception. He's not sure why people think spring water is so clean. Henry thinks that a good number of the elements, metals, and gases down there should stay where they are, untouched, far away from drinking water supplies. They shouldn't be dredged up to the modern world above. They belong in the dark interior. Arsenic and radon are down there. These poisons and radioactive materials are dangerous for people, and for all living things, for that matter. The quality of water coming from this well remains to be seen.

The water here probably flows from the same water source that feeds an aquifer. Henry thinks about the fact that this aquifer is the very same one that leads to the city water supply. In fact, he relies on it at home. All of New York City depends on this particular watershed, over eight million people: more than one and a half million in Manhattan, nearly a million and a half in the Bronx, two and a half million in Brooklyn where he lives, well over two million in Queens and half a million in Staten Island. This may be something he does have in common with the people here, the source of his water.

The front door opens. A sturdy older woman appears, startling Henry. She wears her hair in long silver braids she has wrapped around her head like a crown. The woman stares silently at him.

"Hello. Good afternoon," Henry says, and he smiles.

The woman doesn't respond. Maybe it isn't a good afternoon for her, but that's what people say, or are supposed to say. *Good afternoon*. He wonders why the things he says to people don't seem to make sense to them.

Henry adjusts his glasses. He feels his throat tighten. He's been to many other sites. He understands what happens in the communities after a site is leased for shale gas drilling. People become suspicious. People become dissatisfied. They fear the drilling rigs that go up around them. They resent the new roads and pipes crisscrossing their fields and forests. They hate the pits built for the hazardous wastes flowing back out of the sites. They file complaints after the fracking begins because of the noise, the incessant glare of industrial lights, the clouds of air pollution, the smell from the volatile organic compounds—VOCs—like the chemicals benzene and toluene in the air.

Most people can't stand the smog from the thousands of truck trips for the millions of gallons of water hauled in for each frack of a gas well, and a well may be fracked a dozen different times. Some people say they can't sleep. Others can't breathe, their children get sick, and their pets die. When the methane leaks begin, people worry about the explosions. Henry worries about that too, even though he is only passing through to do a job.

The complaints come in and Henry is hired to go and run tests. If the test results show chemical or gas contamination, then water is brought in from somewhere else. Methane meters are installed. People are told to avoid any kind of open flame. The scenario is predictable, and it happens over and over again, site after site.

In the doorway, Henry tries to see the interior of the house around the old woman. She appears to be mute. He looks at her expressionless face and her limp hands hanging down at her sides. He thinks she may be mentally ill, schizophrenic maybe. Alternatively, the problem could be simply that she doesn't speak English.

He wonders whether this family has plans to leave or if they will stay and fight. Many of the people he's spoken with here hope to leave. Others want to make money, but then later they want the energy company doing the gas drilling to get out. Henry thinks people generally don't know *what* they want. They certainly don't know what's good for them. Residents may move out, move on, thinking that they have left problems of the future behind them. Or at least, they have given the problems to those unfortunate neighbors who could not afford to move, those who did not lease or sell. People like the Smiths.

"Oma, who is it?" Henry hears a girl call from inside the house, in perfect English.

Oma closes the front door firmly and locks it behind her. She turns to the dining room and watches Beth at the table. Beth's laptop is open in front of her.

"Who came by, Oma?" Beth studies her grandmother's somber face for a moment. She calls to her mother, "Maman. Door."

Beth hears someone knock again, louder.

"Maman! Can you get the door? Da's outside working. He can't get it," Beth bellows.

Charlotte emerges from the bedroom. She frowns at the bright light in the dining room. "I've got a headache. Don't yell," she says.

"Door," Beth says and turns back to her schoolwork.

"I heard you. Can you turn off the light? So bright..."

"It's not on, just sunny today. Door, Maman."

Oma stands at the back of the room watching them. She leans against the wall.

"*Damn it!*" Charlotte walks over slowly. She unlocks and opens the door. When she sees Henry, she pulls back.

"What are you doing out here?" she asks him.

"A report about a cat," Henry says. "Testing for..." he points to his backpack.

He stands in the open doorway, momentarily confused. She looks completely different in the sunlight here than when he last saw her, in town, a few nights ago. He was not expecting to recognize let alone actually know anyone at the property.

"Charlotte?"

2:30 PM

Oma hisses like a threatening cat at Henry as he steps inside the house. She spits noisily in his direction. Henry is surprised that neither Charlotte nor the girl seems to notice the old woman's odd behavior.

"Oma, want to make tea?" Beth asks gently.

Oma leaves the room, padding noiselessly into the kitchen.

Beth observes their visitor. Tall, thin, middle-aged. He wears his black hair short and trim, has nice glasses, a pressed shirt. How do he and Maman know each other? Beth has no idea. He smells of something sharp, basil possibly, and some kind of fragrant wood. Cedar or sandalwood. She isn't sure what it is, but she likes it.

Charlotte regards Henry coldly. "Ah, yes, of course. We filed a complaint. Those come to you?"

Henry nods helplessly. *We filed a complaint*—that's one of the things people always say. Of course they did; that's why he's here. Although he can describe the situation and speculate as to the cause, he cannot fix any of their problems, not ever. He silently curses his profession, one that taught him to describe what he cannot change.

He looks over at the pretty girl at the table. He wonders whether the cat was her pet.

"Well then, Dr. Berger, I suppose we could sit in the kitchen," Charlotte suggests. She sounds exhausted. "My mother-in-law is making tea."

Henry hesitates. "You're not using a flame, are you?"

"Of course not. The stove's electric. And the water's brought in. We had to switch over. Didn't they tell you, those...people you work for?"

Henry follows her, speechless. He's not sure he even wants to describe and report on what might be found in Charlotte's home. He would rather not know anything at all about her home, including what's in the water. He won't want to tell her, he's quite sure, once he does know.

Beth continues to go through her science homework. She searches out definitions on Google for the words Mr. Heller gave her. She finds most of them on a government Website, Centers for Disease Control, CDC. Searching for descriptions of the chemical effects on people, she finds the best ones on a site for children's doctors, the

American Academy of Pediatrics, AAP. Beth types out her notes quickly in her own words.

Arsenic is a deadly poison. It comes from the ground in the rock deep below the earth's surface. *Arsenic* contaminates wells, mostly very deep wells, all over the world after mining shakes up the rock. In Bangladesh, nearly all the water is contaminated with arsenic. She's not clear on why that is.

She looks over at the water drum in the corner of their dining room. She's not sure where that water comes from, if it's from deep wells or not. She wonders if it has *arsenic* in it.

Benzene is a chemical found near volcanoes and fires, also around places that make plastics. It's flammable, something like gasoline. When breathed in, it's poisonous to people's bones, their bone marrow, to be specific. *Benzene* causes cancer, leukemia. It also makes you feel tired, have headaches, even pass out, most likely from blood problems like anemia.

For pregnant women and the baby inside, *benzene* is a poison that makes the baby underweight and delays their bones from forming. She isn't sure what a delay in bones forming would lead to, but it sounds terrible. She can't imagine what that would look like—a baby without bones?

The structure of *benzene* is a circle of carbon atoms. The chemist, named Kekulé, who described the structure of the *benzene* carbon ring, daydreamed of a snake eating its own tail in a circle, a famous illustration. She's seen that some people use the symbol as a tattoo. Beth is pleased, remembering how Mr. Heller encouraged her to think about going into science. Medical illustration, he suggested, to use both her natural gifts in arts and sciences. She would like to discover something and draw it too, like they say Kekulé did.

Beth hears Maman crying in the kitchen. She thinks it must be about the cat.

The whole family loved their pet cat, of course. Beth can't remember when they didn't have her around. They called her Cherrie, meaning *dear one*. No one loved her the same way Maman did. Losing Cherrie was terrible for her. The gray shorthair cat was truly Maman's pet. She was her little love. She was her weakness. Cherrie slept on her bed, played at her feet, followed her every step. When Maman went out, Cherrie curled up on whatever piece of Maman's worn clothing she could find or pull down, and napped, waiting for her return.

Maman always said that attachment was a bad thing. Losing Cherrie certainly showed why she thought that way.

Oma emerges from the kitchen and slinks by the dining room table. She climbs the stairs silently. Ever since Cherrie died, Oma doesn't speak. Not a word. Beth is the only one in the family who seems to understand her. She watches Oma carefully, and noticing each little motion, expression, tries to decipher Oma's new body language.

Sometimes Beth imagines that it wasn't Cherrie but Oma who died. She suspects that the cat's soul is inside of Oma's body, hovering silently around their home.

Oma has become restless. She acts like she wants to be loved by the family, but at the same time wants to be free of this life.

Death makes you free, Beth thinks. *Cherrie is free now.*

Beth presses on her forehead with her fingers and tries to concentrate. Only two words are done on her list, seven to go.

Carcinogen is any chemical that causes cancer in animals or people. She wonders whether plants get cancer. She suspects they do, thinking of the bulbous forms on the trunks of some of the older trees, like the oak in front of the house. A *carcinogen* can come from nature or be manmade. She wonders who would want to make that. The idea seems gross, perverse really. The things that science people will do are unbelievable to her.

Ethyl benzene is flammable, toxic, and it comes from gasoline vapors. *Ethyl benzene* has to be stored in a certain way, or it can cause fires or explode. *Ethyl benzene* is similar to benzene and can poison the development of a baby inside. It can wreck a person's or animal's nerves.

Beth hears the visitor's steps coming out of the kitchen. He wears good hiking boots, but she thinks he may not be used to them yet. Dr. Berger, Maman had called him. Beth wonders what kind of a doctor he is. She thinks maybe he knows about these things, the chemicals, but she doesn't want to ask him.

"I'll need a sample of the soil, and the water outside, too. You have a body of water behind the house?" he asks Maman.

"We have a pond," she says.

Beth tries to block them out. She enters *"heavy metals"* in the Internet search box. For this phrase many results lead to music and some to writing. Beth clicks on science-related sites. *Heavy metals* are chemicals that can be good in trace amounts, like iron. Only a little bit more of them and the heavy metals become poisonous. *Arsenic* is one of them; lead and mercury are two others. People poisoned by *heavy metals* get emotional, tired, nauseous, sick.

"I can show you where the stream is, too, farther back behind our place," Maman says to the intruder.

Beth looks up. She watches Maman: *emotional, tired, nauseous, sick*. Maybe the cat's death was not what depressed her. Maybe Maman was simply poisoned by some kind of heavy metal.

Beth keeps searching. *Mercury*, a planet, of course, is also a chemical that looks like liquid silver. It comes out of volcanoes, power plants, and from places where people mine fuels. *Mercury* is toxic to living things. The poison gets concentrated in plants and animals bodies. *Mercury* poisoning can come from eating toxic fish.

Beth has firsthand experience with fish being poisoned, from the time that their stream went bad. That was three months ago. She shakes of the haunting memory.

Methane is an explosive contaminant that is found around mines. "Meth" certainly is familiar here, a drug, but she thinks that's probably something different. A science site says that people keep track of *methane* with meters. This is to prevent fires and explosions at home and poisoning from contaminated drinking water.

She remembers seeing a meter over at the twins Mark and Matt's house when she visited them with Da. She wonders whether the meter was for *methane.* She hopes her friends don't have *methane* in their water.

She searches the word *radioactivity.* This causes mutations. It comes from deep within the earth. *Radioactivity* is used in research to create new mutants. There it is again, a note about making mutants. She wonders why anyone would want to get a mutation on purpose. The thought seems terrible to her.

Beth remembers an unusual butterfly she found by the forest in the tall ferns. The wings were shorter than others she'd seen, and they curled. She was amazed when the butterfly let her pick it up without escaping. But then, maybe it could not fly. Maman was not pleased when Beth brought the creature home.

"A mutant," Maman had said.

That was when Beth began the drawings. When she made the mutant into something artistic, it stopped frightening her. Then the mutant became interesting.

Beth is almost finished with the assignment now. *Selenium* is named for the moon, in Greek. *Selenium* comes from ores and mining. In large amounts, *selenium* contaminates water and is toxic to animals and people. Fingernails fall off, hair falls out. Fingers and toes go numb. Gross, she thinks. So that one's also a poison.

She scans for the keywords in the news excerpts and highlights them in yellow: "*Methane* bubbling up in streams...Five homes saturated with *methane* pose explosion risks...Well blowout in a State Forest releases tens of thousands of gallons of toxic hydrofracking fluids...Millions awarded to three families for *methane* migration to local water supply...Natural gas well leaks diesel fuel into a wetland...Public town well explodes...Gas well explodes, burns for two weeks following *methane* leak into groundwater," and she stops reading.

Lots of bad news is about *methane*. Nauseating, Beth thinks. If Maman has been reading the same news Mr. Heller provided to the class, it's no wonder she seems depressed.

Beth continues reading. "Tap water turns brown following toxic wastewater leak into an artesian well...Pond turns pink...Stream turns blood-red...High levels of *arsenic* found in water on a farm where sudden death of livestock was reported...*Arsenic* detected in water at two thousand times over the limit. *Ethylbenzene, mercury,* and *selenium* found in soil surface beside natural gas well...Explosion at site that pressurizes natural gas from the Marcellus Shale...Cattle deaths reported where fracking water overflow into ponds found to contain *heavy metals* and *radioactivity*...*Arsenic* found at over six thousand times allowed levels on a property where wastewater caught fire and exploded."

Beth stops. Six thousand times more than the allowed levels? She can't stand to read any more. That these news items are near the area she calls home seems horrible to her.

She goes to the back window and looks out where Da is splitting wood. Off to the side, she sees a stranger, a young man, standing by the barn. He seems to be watching their horse. Beth returns to her laptop and quickly finishes the assignment.

She types: *We should know about these new words because they describe things in the world around us that can harm us, our loved ones, and other living things.*

Beth races to the back window again and watches the young man. She wonders what he's doing out there. He's not very tall and has loose brown curls. Not a safe place for a stranger to be, out by the barn—no, not at all. She pulls on a jean jacket and boots and heads out the back door. She runs to the barn.

"Hey Da," she calls as she passes by her father.

He looks up at her and smiles and then goes to get another log. He sets it upright on the chopping block and swings the heavy ax over his shoulder in one smooth arc. The wood splits with a snap.

Beth reaches the young man before he realizes she is coming.

"Hey! Not a good place for you to be." She points to her Da. "He doesn't know you. I'll say you're lost, but you should go."

"Right," Adrian says.

She smiles at him and he sees that her teeth are small and even, like a row of little pearls. Adrian hears the big man split another log with a sharp crack.

"Are you?" She asks.

"Am I what?"

"Lost."

Adrian laughs. "I guess I must be."

"Well, if you are, or you ever get lost, follow the stream. Comes from somewhere, goes to somewhere else. Then you can't be lost anymore."

Adrian watches the log splitting. "Is he dangerous or something?"

"Not to me. Can be, though, if he doesn't know you. He doesn't like strangers. Wouldn't want to find out, if I were you."

"Really? Hey, why is he doing that?"

Beth looks over at Da. "What, cutting wood?"

Adrian nods.

"Don't you know anything? You cut wood for the stove, silly."

"Right. We don't use wood for stoves where I live."

"You're not from around here?"

"No. Don't those wood stoves give off toxic fumes in the house?"

She smiles at him. He doesn't know a thing about them out here. "We don't have a wood stove either anymore. He cuts the wood for later. Da builds houses. You need wood for that too."

"He mentioned that."

She frowns, momentarily confused. "He actually spoke to you?"

Adrian nods. He is charmed by her. "Yes, he did." Adrian turns behind him and touches the horse's velvety nose gently with the palm of his hand. He's never touched a horse before. He is amazed at the softness of the gentle animal. "Beautiful horse. She's yours?"

"Maman's."

"Your mother's?"

Beth nods. "Her name's Jolie. Means *pretty*."

"Sweet. You ride?"

"Of course. So, you came here with that man? The man who does the testing?"

"My dad."

"He's Dr. Berger, isn't he?"

Adrian nods and he wonders how she knows his father's name.

"I draw," she says, and she reaches out to pat Jolie on her neck.

"What kinds of things do you draw? No, let me guess. Pretty horses?"

She laughs. "No. More beautiful things." She whispers, "*Mutants!*"

She looks over at her father. He's watching them.

Adrian says, "I'd like to see your artwork. Like they say, there's no great beauty without some strangeness..."

"Who says?" she asks.

The horse swishes her tail and swats her flank, dislodging flies that hover around her.

"Poe. Edgar Allan Poe," Adrian whispers.

Beth is happy to hear a name she knows. Poe is one of her favorite writers, though Maman doesn't much like him.

Adrian cries out, "Ah!" He slaps his leg. A dark spot of blood is leaking through his jeans on his thigh.

"Horsefly!" Beth says and she waves her hand at a large gray fly.

"Painful. Damn it!" Adrian rubs his leg.

Beth laughs. "He was eating you. They're possessed, flies are, from the world of the dead. Go. Go; act like you're looking for something. Looking for your scientist dad. Go!" Beth runs off, back to the house.

As she passes by her Da again, she stops and says, "I think he's just lost. I told him to go. See, he's going now."

Da leans on the ax and watches the young man leave.

3 PM

Henry picks up bits of dirt and places them in small vials to analyze for chemicals later. He's surprised to find that some of the plants growing at the Smith place are the same as the ones that grow behind his house in Brooklyn. Growing in lush patches, he recognizes the medicinal plant Echinacea, a purple coneflower that looks like a huge daisy. He's too cautious to use the wild plant himself, but at home he keeps capsules of Echinacea he purchased at the health food store.

The air is rich with the scent of roses that, at first, he thinks is Charlotte's perfume, but then he sees the resplendent flowers dipping forward on slim stems. Of course she would have roses.

He knows he must explain himself to her. She walks silently beside him. He avoids the moment. Where can he begin? They didn't talk about work the other times they had met. She's certain to ask him what he does now. As a rule, he avoids talking about his job with people if he doesn't actually have to work with them. Henry hates controversy.

When they met before, he and Charlotte talked about music, the songs she was writing, or books. Even love. They drank. He read her poetry—Neruda sometimes, or Paz—and watched her fall asleep. He asked her to read him something in French. She was a natural storyteller. She liked reading from Baudelaire's work, and certainly no one described intoxication quite like Baudelaire, which was fitting. Henry enjoyed the sound of her voice, no matter what she read. He couldn't say that he loved Charlotte, but he did love being with her. No question about that at all.

"I started coming out to Brindle after the fish kill," Henry explains, and he feels his throat tightening up. Anxiety, he's sure. He tries to swallow and he can't. He's terrified that he'll have a panic attack right here in the middle of nowhere. The thought fills him with dread.

"Come when things die? That's what you do?" she asks.

Henry smiles apologetically.

"I did not know that about you when we met," she says.

"You didn't know anything about me. You were drunk when we met." The minute the words are out, he wishes he could take them back. He feels a twisting pain in his chest and like he might faint. He wants to sit down, but they keep walking. He has work to complete.

"I'm sorry—"

Charlotte cuts him off, "Don't be. It's very likely I was, and that was a long time ago. I've stopped drinking now, you know. It's not allowed."

Henry isn't sure what she means, but not drinking could only be a good thing for her and for him too, for that matter.

Trudging along, he's afraid he'll get lost if they go too far from the house. He tries to focus on something concrete, on Charlotte. He remembers how he met her.

She sat alone in the full sun on a wooden bench in front of a Brindle neighborhood bar, early in the spring. He remembers that she was wearing a black ballet leotard under faded jeans, with black boots. When he passed by, she asked him if they allowed nude sunbathing there. He had no idea. He was sure she was drunk. He told her that the thought of her naked was too much for him to even try to imagine. It was, but he did. He asked her if she wouldn't like to go get something to eat. She said she would, and things went on from there to where they are now, lovers but not really friends.

"Why did they send you out here?" Charlotte asks.

He remembers the disaster with the fish that had disturbed so many people. He feels nauseous thinking about it, but that could be the anxiety. He knows now, after the analysis was completed and the reports written, that they all died in droves on account of the high salt in the wastewater released from the drilling sites.

"The energy company had to have someone look into it. Three months ago. That was the first time I came out here, wasn't it?"

"You work for them, then?" she asks.

"Not exactly *for* them, but they do pay me by the job." He is short of breath. He starts to sweat. He's afraid he won't be able to control the situation of being with her in her own environment. He is a stranger here, trespassing. He badly wants to leave.

Charlotte looks at Henry carefully from head to toe. She's not surprised that he works for the energy company, but she wouldn't have guessed it if he hadn't said. She imagined that he was a professor, of literature, possibly. What a disappointment.

"So, you're a science whore," she says.

He starts coughing and nearly chokes. *Science whore!*

She watches and doesn't feel the least bit sorry for him. "And so with your paid work, your science, you come to look at us, come and change everything you see?" she asks.

"No, only to look." He thinks about what he said and wonders if it's true. Nothing can be observed without changing it in some way. This is a conflict that scientists like him face in their work every day, if they think about it. Mostly they don't think about it.

She smiles sweetly. "You won't take our poetry away from us, will you?"

He frowns and can't formulate a response. He hyperventilates. He looks away from her over at the line of trees bordering the forest and tries to slow his breathing down to a normal rate. A breeze makes him feel suddenly chilled. He begins to shake.

She continues, "No. Not you. Leave us our sad songs, our poems, our magic. What kind of person are you, really, Henry?"

Charlotte remembers discussing people and animals with him not so long ago. The three types he settled on were wolves, shepherds, and sheep. Henry said he thought you could put anyone in one of these categories based on their profession.

A sort of balance existed in the world, in his mind, where they all needed one another. Even wolves needed shepherds. To keep the flock healthy and get rid of weak or sick sheep, the shepherds needed the wolves too. Henry thought of oil and gas men as wolves, people like Officer Joe as shepherds, and most everyone else, well, as sheep, or so he said. He was somewhat like a sheep himself, following along without trying to change the course of things around him. They had had a difference of opinion about the whole animal analogy thing.

She thought that a person who might have been a shepherd by nature could be cast in a role as one of the wolves. That person would become unhappy, feel out of place, and would have a terribly uncomfortable life trying to adjust, unable to fit in with the others. She told Henry he was probably one of those. Or even this could happen: A wolf could find himself accidentally in the midst of a herd of sheep, lost but not hungry nor hunting. A cruel person by nature, bored with his life. That was also possible. David might be one of these, she imagined. Overall, she didn't think that Henry's animal analogy was a very good one. But she remembers that she had made him laugh, which she enjoyed.

Henry doesn't know how to describe himself. He decides to stick with his work identity today instead of animal stories. He cannot really hide what he does any longer. "I'm a geologist, a soil scientist; I look at the chemicals in the dirt, in the water. I'd like to have a look at your pond, if you don't mind." He spits it out and takes a deep breath.

"What do you look for in the water, what chemicals?"

He shrugs.

"Things like phenol?" she asks.

He nods and wonders where she heard of phenol.

"And animals? You look at them too?"

"The chemicals I test for do affect animals—that's true. But I'm not really a biologist, not by training. My background's in geology and chemistry."

"And the people? These things affect the people, you know. What about us?" she asks.

Henry thinks about it for a moment. He simply doesn't know enough about that to say. "When I came up after the fish were in the news, you know, the press started to get their hands into it—"

"Shouldn't they?"

"No! No, not at all. That was terrible, irresponsible. It upsets people even more to have something like mass death publicized in the newspaper, to have that go up online. Awful."

He wonders whether coming out here will contaminate him. He feels suddenly overwhelmed with fear, a fear of death.

Charlotte says, "I remember. We did call the television stations too, you know, but they never came. It didn't end with the one time. No, and it will never end. From time to time, the fish still die. And they get tumors. The fish, they get cancer, you know. They get cancer like people do. Fish have a life cycle. People have a life cycle. The earth does too. Tell me, Henry; tell me that it's not dying here."

He can't say it. He doesn't want to elaborate on what was found after the analysis of the site. With every job he completes, he documents the ways the earth—or life on earth as he knows it—is dying. Yet he presses on, he studies it, he reports it. He survives.

Charlotte remembers how the stream water had turned brown. First came the smell. Then a few dead fish, then hundreds, thousands, tens of thousands. Salamanders, too, died by the thousands. Finally the dead could not be counted. To her, this period three months ago seemed apocalyptic.

Henry and Charlotte circle the pond behind the barn. He crouches down to take a sample of the water. He looks back over his shoulder at her. She stands on the narrow strip of land between this pond and the swamp next door. *The earth has a life cycle*, she had said and it repeats in his mind. This beautiful woman he had enjoyed so completely in a different setting— it's as if he's seeing her for the first time, here, in her natural environment. The place is rich, earthy, messy. Charlotte is slight, lost in thought, vulnerable. Seeing her in the middle of it, all at once he wishes he had understood her more when he met her. He's afraid he wasted their time. He knows she will not be interested in him here. She will not love him now. No, not at all, he thinks. It is over.

Charlotte is motionless, staring down at something. She slowly covers her mouth with her hands.

"What?" Henry puts the water sample in his backpack. He walks up the side of the pond, slipping in the mud. "Damn it!" he whispers. He struggles along toward Charlotte, wiping muck from his new hiking boots on the tall grass.

"He's killed it," she whispers.

"Who?"

"David," she says.

David, he thinks. That must be her husband's name. Henry looks toward where she is staring and he sees it. The enormous snapping turtle with a hole in its neck is dead at her feet. Its shell spans a meter in diameter. The earth beneath the lifeless, prehistoric body is a deathbed soaked in blood.

"God, Charlotte, come away from there. Get away from it!"

She seems stunned. He takes her gently by the arm and leads her slowly past the pond through the fields. They stop at the edge of the forest and sit together side by side on a fallen tree. He's exhausted from the panic attack and then the bizarre scene at the pond. Henry has never seen a snapping turtle before and certainly was not expecting to see a dead one. He wants to go home. He feels unhinged.

Henry and Charlotte sit together in silence for a long time. It seems like forever. He feels acutely uncomfortable. He's afraid she's in shock. But he tries to make conversation that will pass for normal, even though he feels crazy.

"Your family owns the house and the property behind it up to here?" he asks.

"From here on," Charlotte waves toward the dense trees, "that part is not ours. But up to the forest, this is ours. My family came from Louisiana." She smiles at him. "We're French, did you know?"

"You mentioned that. Your family place is the only property not leased or sold in the whole area."

"Yes. The landsman came, you know. A silly man, a stupid man, I think. He must hate his job. But he does his job, and people let go of things. They let go of the land too easily. And then they hang on to other things that are totally useless. What a life. We own this land, we use it. Why would we let it go?"

"Money. Leasing brings in a lot of money, Charlotte." Henry takes her left hand in both of his. It seems weightless inside his grasp. Her skin feels like silk-satin stretched in tiny folds around her bones. "You know it's about the money; why are we even talking about this?"

He wants to protect her from all of this, from toxic water and contaminated land. Most of all, he wants to protect her from men with guns who kill snapping turtles. He wants to be her hero, or at least her friend. He fingers her rings gently before she pulls her hand away.

"Not everyone needs more money," she says. "I don't. My family doesn't. You might not realize it, but we have our riches here, and we have our peace. We have the forest, the wildflowers. They're not weighed the same way your treasures are, not bought and sold. So you don't recognize the value of them. What's the use in talking about it? Let's walk so you can do your work. The stream isn't far from here."

A red-winged blackbird chatters in tall reeds as they pass by. It calls others that fly at Henry's head, and one brushes him with its wings. He cringes and another blackbird dives, batting him around his face, hitting his glasses with wildly flapping wings.

"We're near one of their nests," Charlotte says. "Keep walking and they'll see that you're no threat. They'll leave you alone then."

She stops to look at him. "Or maybe you are, and then they won't stop."

She throws her hands up. "*Ah!* I just had a realization. Maybe Cherrie ate one of them, the bad fish, the ones that died. *Mon Dieu!* Is it possible?"

"Who?" Henry asks.

"Cherrie! My little cat," she says.

Henry is horrified. Toxic elements are taken in and filtered and then more concentrated in fish that live in contaminated water. Heavy metals would build up in the fish, of course. Eating the fish or anything else that comes from the land here would be poisonous. Living here seems like a definite health hazard. "You let her outside?"

"What do you mean, *let* her?" Charlotte asks.

He runs the phrase over and over in his mind. *You let her outside.* It's what people say, don't they? His throat tightens up but he tries to communicate. "Your cat, she ran around outside the house?"

Charlotte frowns at him. "How do you not let a cat out? You can't make a cat do anything, or not do anything. They do whatever they want to do; they go wherever they want to go, freely."

She leads him toward the stream. "Cats are like children," she says. "They go everywhere, anywhere. Impossible to keep track of them."

As she walks under the trees, her steps are silenced by the soft bed of pine needles. She looks like a big cat herself, Henry thinks, a thin one—a cheetah, maybe. The forest is a place she knows and loves but he is a stranger here. He feels a pang of envy because she belongs but he doesn't. He trips over exposed tree roots and fallen branches as he scrambles along behind her.

He hears a high and penetrating whistle from the trees, sharp and clear. It repeats and seems to be following them. "What *is* that?" he asks.

Charlotte looks up through the trees, tilting her head. She sees a flash of brilliant red. "The cardinal. He's following us."

"Is that a good thing?"

She shrugs and continues on steadily. A cardinal follows her all around the place when she goes for walks. Mornings, it comes to her bedroom window, calling insistently in the high, pure whistle. She always thinks of the cardinal's visits as a sign that she's trapped. She imagines the bird is calling her to come out of her cage, the house, to be free again.

Henry says, "You should be more careful with your pets out here. Where I live, we don't let cats out of the house, not ever. Dogs, yes, but always on a leash. And kids, forget it. When they're small, they don't go out on the street either, not without an adult."

He's as troubled now about Charlotte's dead cat as he was by the fish disaster earlier in the spring. He knows that animals are sentinels for the poisoning of the land. Wild animals are more exposed to the elements, land and water, even the air. They are less protected, less sheltered. Death of pets, livestock, and wild populations of animals sounds an alarm for any ecosystem.

Charlotte stops. She leans over, cupping a wildflower in her palm. "Do you know what this is?"

He doesn't.

"A bleeding heart," she says and smiles, her eyes half closed. "Columbine, we call them. They're magical." Columbine in the forest, waiting here bleeding, she thinks. Waiting for her love to return so she can fly away from here. That is how the mythical story of the columbine goes. She's composing a new song about the flower.

Who will be her love? Not David, not now. Since he came back from his last deployment to Afghanistan he has wanted nothing to do with her. Not Henry, the empty person that she sees before her now. Maybe Joe, or maybe not. Where will she go—New Orleans, France? She has no idea.

Henry looks at the plant closely. The unopened flower in Charlotte's hand does in fact look like a miniature human heart. He's quite sure he has never seen this kind of flower before today.

Charlotte continues on ahead, making no sound with her footsteps in front of him.

"Who's the young lady back at the house?" Henry asks.

She wishes he would not speak, but he can't seem to be quiet. "My daughter. She's my daughter, Beth."

Henry stops in his tracks. He thinks Charlotte can't be more than thirty herself. A daughter—he had no idea.

4 PM

"We're close to where the nature preserve starts now," Charlotte says to Henry. "The magic begins here. Can you feel it?" She suspects he probably can't. She walks here daily, looking for something, peace mostly. The forest gives her more than she comes looking for, every time. She thinks that she will not want to leave Brindle, not ever, no matter what Dr. Miller says. She was born here, and she imagines that she will die here.

She listens. "I hear the trees whispering sometimes. They don't talk to everyone. Or maybe they do, but not everyone listens. Do you hear them?" She looks at Henry carefully and wonders what he notices here. "Henry?"

No, he doesn't hear anything but the wind and the piercing whistle of the cardinal following them. The forest awakens deep memories for some. The sounds that echo in Henry's thoughts are not those he loves from long ago. They are more recent ones that torment him. The high-pitched sound coming out of the small boy who stood by the bus this morning—that repeats in his mind. He hears the boy screaming, looking at the bus driver's body. Henry wants an escape from his uncontrolled, random thoughts. Today is the first day he's ever seen a dead turtle. And now his lover—who has a grown daughter—thinks the trees are talking. What's next?

"So, what kinds of things do trees say?" he asks.

She closes her eyes, tilting her head up. The ancient trees are the deep earth's language for speaking to the universe. The earth communicates through trees to the animals and to the birds living above—and to the very heavens. The trees draw the earth's water up from the ground. Then breathing, they return it to the air for the clouds and the blessed rain that falls to begin the cycle anew. She thinks of the thin layer of living things as a fragile space between earth's molten rock core and the frozen outer universe of stars. The thin layer is like her own life here—precious, finite.

She listens, hushed.

"I'm here. We're here," she says.

Charlotte looks so light that Henry thinks a breeze could carry her away from him.

"The trees say that?" he asks.

She nods.

"In English? Or maybe it's French."

She gives him a disgusted look, turning down the corners of her mouth, and frowns. "Not a sound; it's a feeling, like a thought."

"They say things? I'm sorry. I mean, they *think* things like that? *We're here*?"

"Yes. Trees are very...in the moment, you know."

"That's ridiculous."

She smiles at him. "Each of these trees was born. Each of them will die, just like everyone you know and everyone you've ever known will die. But right now, they are in the moment."

Henry tries to focus on the work at hand. He can't. *We're here.* He hears it repeated in her voice. Her words are inside him.

Charlotte living in this contaminated place seems terrible to him. And with a teenage daughter—even worse. *Everyone you've ever known will die,* she said. He feels like he can't breathe again and he tries to relax his throat muscles. He knows of ten drill pads and a place that stores toxic fracking fluid, all within a mile of the property. A wastewater storage pit sits on the north side past the family barn. In the rain, the toxic runoff must flow down the hill into the pond from the neighbor's marsh and toward the stream.

I'm here, we're here; her words repeat in his head. He remembers that this is why he fell in love with Charlotte, or with seeing her. She says things that actually mean something to him. Her ideas touch him at the same time that they disturb him. Henry sometimes falls in love with people who disturb him. They awaken the part of him that sleeps through the numbing repetition of his days. They stir him, move him.

Watching Charlotte here, he remembers the case of wastewater found dumped in the forest. It was hundreds of thousands of gallons. Another time, fracking fluids spouted into the forest like a geyser when the drill hit gas, before the company got it under control. Company workers pleaded guilty to felony. They were fined. The facts pierce through like stabbing pinpricks in his mind, murdering his softer thoughts. Each of these problems happened not so far from here, in Charlotte's world.

Reports came out about issues with animals at different times after the dumping was discovered. Cattle had breakdowns in their motor skills and died suddenly. Stillbirths and mutant calves were reported.

The situation in Brindle is a chemist's nightmare come to life. Some chemists get to see snakes eating their tails and discover benzene's structure. Some discover new compounds or elements and name them. Henry sees poisoned fish with tumors, mutant calves born blind with white eyes, and discovers nothing at all. He feels betrayed by science.

He chokes, coughs, and tries to catch his breath. He looks up at the tall trees and the fragments of sky above them. He wonders, what will happen to these trees? Will they turn brown? What will happen to this little family he plunged himself directly into, three months ago now? Will they get sick?

He wants to love Charlotte, her family, and even the forest around them. He can't because of the endless war his thoughts wage on his emotions, drowning them. The thoughts always win. He is left grappling with fact after disturbing fact cascading like a waterfall through an empty place inside him. He wants to love, but because he can't, he despises his love.

The heart is a muscle, he reminds himself. It is a stupid, mute muscle that reacts to low blood sugar, to fatigue. The feeling of despair is nothing more than the effect of hormones and other compounds in the blood surrounding the muscle of the heart. Yet, he feels despair.

Here, today, the family's dead pet cat could have resulted from any number of things. He may find that they had a gas leak. He remembers the song Adrian was singing in the morning right before the accident: *Water, clean water, you can't drink gasoline.* The tests might show salts, metals, radiation, toxins from wastewater exposure to the creek, or they might show nothing at all. *Water, clean water*...Henry thinks that possibly the soil samples will be fine, and that the family cat may have simply been old or sick. Maybe it was both old and sick. Old sick things die.

"What happened to your cat, exactly?" he asks. "Charlotte?"

She walks along the stream silently and he thinks she's ignoring him.

"She got weak, my little cat," she says, finally.

Neurotoxicity, he thinks. He notices that the stream water smells faintly sweet. He suspects it may be from the chemical toluene, a contaminant found in this area previously.

"It all happened very suddenly, and then she died," Charlotte says.

"Organs failed, probably." The kidneys or heart may have stopped functioning, he thinks.

She remembers but cannot speak about it.

She stayed up all night with Cherrie, holding her, bringing her water. Every time the little cat drank, she vomited the water back out of her body. Charlotte was cleaning around her, listening to her cry, holding her again.

They sat in a chair by the window together. Charlotte wrapped a long scarf around Cherrie, binding the cat to her chest so she wouldn't fall, in case sleep came over her. It didn't.

At the end Cherrie howled repeatedly, curling her head sideways each time, trying to escape from the pain. No amount of petting, softly whispered words, or songs could calm her. She howled louder and louder for hours and then at about five in the morning she was still. Her breathing became slow and shallow. She looked like she was smiling with her eyes closed. And then the pause. Her head lifted, Charlotte kissed her, and she drifted away. She was gone. No, she cannot speak about this.

Henry considers another suspect in the pet's death: ethylene glycol contamination. This is the stuff of common antifreeze, one of many toxins used in gas drilling nearby. He runs through details about other recent reports. People describe that their pets lose hair. A complaint came in last week about a stillborn litter. His thoughts jump from one dataset to another.

He feels lost. He looks at Charlotte steadily, trying to focus his attention on something real. He hopes she leads him back safely. He wants to collect the stream sample and then leave as soon as possible. He is now, in fact, completely lost.

She says, "What happened with Cherrie was not like from a disease. You know? I had a cat that died from a disease when I was very young."

The memory is distant enough that she can talk about it. She likes telling a story, even a horrible one. "This was before we understood about getting the shots, the vaccinations," she says carefully, "for our animals. I had a cat that caught what they call distemper. It was a virus from the ground, raccoons maybe, very contagious. The veterinarian told us when he came."

"Virus doesn't come from the ground. Virus goes from animal to animal," Henry says.

"This virus, the distemper, it can live on the ground, though, from the other animals who pass by, you know? My cat wouldn't drink. She seemed depressed. Saliva accumulated around her teeth. It thickened like glue. I kept trying to clean her, you know? To clean her mouth so she could drink some water at least. She couldn't. Her little head hung down but she couldn't drink. Her body got stiff. It frightened me to see it. I can tell you, her death was horrible to me. Well, now they all get vaccinations: the cat, the horse, my husband, Beth. We all do."

She stops at the edge of the stream.

"I take care of them," she says. "I love them so much."

He is distressed to hear her say this because he knows she can't really take care of them, not like she would want to. This is one of the things people say that mean nothing—*I take care of them.* They *think* they take care of their families. They can't really guard against what they can't see, can't measure, and don't understand. It simply isn't possible. They can't really take care of their families, not here, not now.

Henry notices that the edges of the rocks along the stream are tinged with red. This discoloration is an ominous sign to him. *Water, clean water*...he takes out his phone and photographs the reddish rocks along the water. The color could be from a toxic metal seeping up from the rock deep below. He wonders whether radiation came up in the water too, along with the metal. He plans to check concentrations of the radioactive element, radon. That test is essential.

He asks, "What did the vet tell you about your cat this time?"

"But, I didn't take Cherrie to the vet."

Henry looks at her as he takes out his supplies for sampling the stream water. He has a vial of the water from the house that he took in the kitchen, and the one from the pond. He wonders whether the stream water will be any different. He gathers the sample so finally, they can go back.

"No? Why not?" he asks.

"What's the point, Henry? My little cat, she was dead already."

"Where is she now?"

"God only knows. In the song of a newborn bird here, I imagine. I don't know."

Henry closes his eyes. *God only knows.* These things people say that mean nothing at all to him. Maddening. "I meant her body, Charlotte," he says.

She leans over the stream bank and runs her hand along the water. She had Cherrie cremated, naturally. The ashes are on her desk in her bedroom and she lights a candle by them each night. She doesn't want to talk about it.

"I wouldn't do that," Henry says, staring at her pretty fingers trailing along in the water. Her wedding rings glint in the fragments of sunlight tracing through the leaves around them.

"You're fairly disgusting, as a person, when you talk about your work," she says. "Disgusting. Did you know that about yourself?"

He shrugs. It is true. He is disgusting. Naturally she would feel that way. He expected she would from the moment she opened the door at the house. He has lost her. But then, he thought he had lost Adrian, that his mother had poisoned the boy's mind against him. Still, Adrian came back to him, miraculously, and seems to love him. Henry knows he is hopelessly bad at predicting the future. He decides not to even try. He has lost Charlotte for now, but possibly not forever.

He puts the samples he's taken away in his backpack and runs through the list of things he might find in them, hundreds of chemicals, dozens of carcinogens. *God only knows* repeats in his head. *God only knows.* Well, Henry does not know, and this time he really does not want to know either, just what exactly is in the water and the ground.

"We can go back," he says.

"Can we?" she asks. "Can you ever go back? I don't think we can," she says sadly, but she leads him back the way they came. They walk side by side out of the forest through the field.

This time the birds ignore Henry. They chatter among themselves in the reeds as if he is not there. He wonders whether, in his emptiness, he may have become invisible to them.

*****

"Hey, where were you?" Adrian calls. He watches his father coming toward the house.

"Collecting water samples," Henry says. He is so relieved to see his son standing there. "Taking pictures. I've got what I needed. I'm done. Adrian, I'm exhausted! Let's go."

"Right. Well, I was out looking at the horse. There's a stream out here?" Adrian asks and his father nods. Adrian makes a note to himself to find the stream and follow it, like the girl said, because maybe he is lost after all.

Adrian smiles at the quiet woman walking beside his father. "Your horse is a beauty. Hi, I'm Adrian."

"I'm Mrs. Smith. Call me Charlotte, Adrian. *Enchantée.*"

Adrian points to the big man who swings the ax over his shoulder and splits a log open. Henry jumps involuntarily.

David sets the ax down, leans back, and stares at the intruders.

"Can I ask you something? Do you know why he's doing that?" Adrian asks.

Charlotte looks where he is pointing. "Doing what?"

"Piling up so much wood. It's amazing." Adrian laughs. "Who does that?"

She shakes her head. "Don't think about it. It doesn't concern you."

Henry cranes his neck to see behind the house. He sees enough split wood to build another entire barn. "You aren't burning firewood, are you? You know you can't burn anything here, nothing at all." Henry says.

Adrian gives him a strange look. This is the same kind of conversation he just had with the girl.

"*Si tu sais.* You worry so much, Henry, and you don't even live here," Charlotte replies. "I'm sorry to leave you both. I have to start cooking now."

Adrian brightens up. "You know that song? '*Si tu sais*,'" he sings. "You say you really know me..."

She tilts her head back, narrows her eyes, and looks at the young man carefully. He's musical, he's interesting. He looks like Henry but shorter, younger, and with curls—lovely curls.

"*Si tu sais*," Adrian prompts.

Charlotte nods slowly. *Is it true, is it over*? She knows the song, better in French than in English. "Yohanna. Her songs are simple, they are good. Yes, I know her, Adrian. You see, as Henry says, we can't burn the wood anymore. No one on this road can. No open fires. Will we ever be able to again? We don't know. My husband..."

She waits on that one word, husband, flooded with a feeling that isn't quite love but is equally painful. "David still cuts the wood. He's waiting for the day when he can burn. Burn it again. The day will come." She tips her head down and walks quickly back inside the house.

David starts over toward them, carrying the ax with him. He meets the father and son at the driveway, near their car.

"I think it's time for you to leave now," David says.

"We're going," Henry emphatically agrees. He backs away with Adrian. They quickly pull out of the driveway of this private place that Henry did not ever want to enter. He is anxious to leave the entire experience at the Smith property behind him. He wishes he had never come.

*****

In the car Adrian asks, "Why can't they burn the wood? What's that about?"

His father stares at the road, driving.

"Are you feeling sick?" Adrian asks.

"Yes. No. In certain places, you can't burn anything. No fires, no flame of any kind. Methane leaks out of the ground here from the rocks. Methane is flammable. A kind of gas. It burns. Explodes."

"Right."

"In some areas, but not everywhere. Some properties are saturated with methane, some are supersaturated. It's dangerous. They didn't teach you about natural gas in school? Fracking? Hydraulic fracturing?"

Adrian shakes his head. No, not that he remembers.

"The house gets an electric stove. And they have the potable water brought in from outside. That's it," Henry says.

"The big guy's a builder," Adrian says. "I was talking to him."

"Really."

"Builds houses out here," Adrian says.

"Is that right." Henry wonders who would want to build here now. The only things he's seen being built in the area are roads, pipelines, and rigs. The temporary man-villages for the workers hardly count. Henry drives, trying to think of something neutral to say to his son.

He asks, "Who's the singer you mentioned?"

"I found her on YouTube. I was so in love with her."

The words echo in his head and he can't stop them. *I was so in love with her.* Was he? He was interested, fascinated by Charlotte for the past three months. *I was so in love with her.* He's unsure it was love.

"Or I thought I was..." Adrian says, and he visualizes the country girl, how she stood in the sunlight beside her beautiful horse, telling him to leave.

"Until today."

5 PM

Mark pours dried food into a stainless-steel bowl for Gabby, the eighty-pound male German shepherd that Mom left behind when she went away for the last time. Mark whistles and Gabby lopes over toward the trailer. The dog stops about ten feet away, waiting. Every time Mark feeds Gabby, he wishes his mother would come back home.

Matt watches his twin brother and says, "I'm hungry."

"Can't expect Gabby to fast; that's not normal," Mark answers.

They walk inside together, leaving Gabby's fresh food outside for him by the side of the trailer. Matt looks at the photo of their mother that they keep on the table in the middle of the room. She looks beautiful dressed in her army uniform—clean, happy, her hair parted on the side and tucked behind her ears. This is the way he remembers her. He badly wants to be like her. He picks up a pair of fresh, clean jeans folded neatly on a chair and pulls them on.

"Almost fit now. But Mark, I'm hungry."

"Don't think about it. Some places in the world they fast one day every week. It's not just us."

"Where?"

"Different places. India, I think. I'm not sure where it was. I read about it. But it's a health thing. Cleans the body. Good for nerve cells, whatever." Mark says. "One day. Just one day, Matt, it won't kill you. Then you'll live longer. That prevention guy says it's good for health."

"I know. I believe him."

Mark looks at his reflection in the full-length mirror that leans against the wall by the entryway. He looks good, lean and fit; his muscles pop out of his T-shirt around his shoulders and upper arms. But then he notices spots on the front of his shirt.

"Damn it." He looks down and sees that the spots are dried blood. "Goddamn moron truck driver. Look! That cretin, he ruined a good shirt." He pulls the shirt out away from him and lets out a long string of curses.

"We'll wash it," Matt says. "Blood comes out in cold water if you don't wait too long. Blood's protein, mostly, so cold water. We'll go down to the stream."

Mark nods. "It's still warm out. We can go for a swim. I need a bath."

"I'll go, if we bring Gabby. Gabby!" Matt calls.

Mark fusses around in the kitchen looking for supplies. "I got soap," he says. "Bring a towel."

Their old German shepherd pads around the corner of the house and stands by the door waiting for them. His food bowl is empty. When the twins come out, Gabby wags his tail slowly.

The twins head out together, walking toward the stream beside their place. Gabby keeps a steady pace about ten yards ahead of them and then waits at the stream. He's a born guard dog.

At the stream edge, Mark pulls off his shirt and scrubs the spots of blood in the flowing water. Matt bathes Gabby, rubbing soap all over his luxurious fur. Gabby suffers the attention silently, his tail down. He stalks into the stream and swims around, holding his head high until the water behind him is clear of soap. Gabby pulls himself out of the water slowly and shakes his dark coat vigorously.

"He's so happy; look at him," Matt says and laughs.

"We shouldn't get soap in the water, probably," Mark says. He's rubbing Gabby dry with the towel.

"That's our only towel. I only brought one," Matt says. "Hey, you think what happened this morning is a problem? They'll blame us?"

"Us? Hell no. Officer Joe went by the school; he'll tell them what happened. He'll vouch for us. The trucker, that's another story. He's going to have all kinds of problems, big ones. Manslaughter probably, something like that. Broken teeth don't mean anything in comparison. Think about it. Old Nan's dead."

"But he's got a job. We don't. No more buildings going up. David won't have anything for us this summer."

Mark ignores him.

Saying David's name reminds Matt of Charlotte and how it smells when she bakes bread or cakes. He tries to put the thought out of his mind.

"Nothing going on but drilling now and I'm sure as hell not going to work for the energy company," Matt rambles, knowing that Mark probably isn't going to respond. "I have to tell you, I'm worried about this morning. I think it could be a problem. We've got to finish school. Infantry won't take us without a diploma. Will they? We're supposed to go for basic combat training. We've got to go to Fort Benning, to Georgia. What if we can't go? God. I wonder what we'll do then."

He's sure that if he brings up Mom, Mark will respond. "Mom, she'd be upset. You know she would."

Mark looks at his brother. "You'll get your diploma and I'll get mine. Joe will take care of Gabby, and we'll go. That's it. Stop worrying."

Mark strips at the edge of the stream, hanging his clothes in a fork of a tree trunk. "She can't get upset anymore, no point in thinking about it like that. Think about her being happy. I do. Mom's happy, Matt. That's how it is now. Permanently happy. Infinitely happy. She will never, ever be upset again." He wades in and swims upstream.

Matt strips and follows his brother in, hooting, "Cold! Man, it's cold."

They both soap up, looking like foaming mummies. They dip under the water, splashing each other when they come back up for air.

The twins sit on the bank, letting their skin dry before they get dressed; they already used the towel on Gabby. Mark leans over the edge of the stream and soaps up the towel, rinses it clean, and rings the water out of it. Matt thinks he twists it impossibly tight between his strong arms, but then it's nearly dry when he flips it in front of him sharply.

"Clothes. What a concept. Us and our clothes. You think we look like idiots?" Matt asks Gabby.

Gabby wags his tail and shakes his fur again, spraying Matt with water droplets.

"I do. I think we look ridiculous. Humans are ridiculous," he sings, laughing. "What a weird word. Ri-dic-u-lous. Ha!"

6 PM

Officer Joe pulls his vehicle over by the Smith property. He expects that the news of Beth vandalizing the gas fracking sites might be a lot for her father to take. Joe dreads being the one to break the news.

He sits for a moment to collect himself before going in to visit with the family. Joe notices how the Smith place is not marred by the gas drilling going on around it, not yet. He wonders how long that will last. The massive oak in the front of the house must be over a hundred years old. It still looks healthy. The eight pear trees that line the side of the house are dense and bright green. Joe sees that the tiny fruits are already growing, hundreds of miniature pears dangling tight and green at the base of each flower that bloomed not so long ago. The trees promise a full crop of pears again this year.

Joe gets out slowly, walks up to the house, and knocks.

Charlotte opens the door. "Hey, Joe. What's going on?" She tips her head back and smiles at him. He's a big man and not quite as cold as David.

A sweet scent of brandy surrounds her after she speaks. Joe sees Beth behind them, sitting at the dining room table. She's working on her laptop.

"Hello, Charlotte." Joe says.

"Wasn't expecting you, but today's full of surprises. Can you stay a minute?" she asks.

"I can."

"Will you eat something?"

"No, but thanks. I have to talk with your husband."

Charlotte turns from the door and Beth thinks she sees a darkness come over her mother.

"David's in the library study; you know where it is," Charlotte says.

Beth quietly picks up her notebook and laptop from the dining room table and heads upstairs. Officer Joe watches her, David's little princess. In that moment he thinks he's never seen anyone more beautiful or more fragile than this girl, not in his entire life.

He walks by the table and stops to look at a bowl of fresh field strawberries, still half full. David says that his daughter calls these "happy strawberries" because they grow wild. He says she thinks the fruit sold in stores is "unhappy" because it sits in boxes separated from the plant. She has a thing about plants; she identifies with them. Joe noticed that from the drawings in her art portfolio too.

One of the things Joe loves about living in Brindle is that some of the women still harvest wild berries—raspberries, blackberries, currants, strawberries. On the table beside the berries is a freshly cut almond cake, brown on the edges and dusted with powdered sugar. The cake smells divine. That Charlotte has been baking is a good sign, Joe thinks.

Entering the study, Joe says, "Got a problem at the drill site today."

He sees that David was reading a historical novel. Now that the construction business is so slow, every time Joe comes by, his friend is reading.

David puts down his book and stands. He is a well-built man who keeps himself in shape and is as tall as Joe. David had two tours in the Gulf. Joe thinks of him as the strongest man he's ever known. Both in the National Guard, they were deployed to the same area of Afghanistan and served together.

They rarely talk about their time over there, but Joe knows that David came home with posttraumatic stress disorder, PTSD. David has a hard time talking with anyone now but soldiers or other guardsmen. Joe came back with nightmares and night sweats himself. Not worse or better off than his friend, but different.

They each lost things that can't ever be replaced, and yet Joe knows that they both would go back, if called.

David says, "That's news? I thought if you came out here, you'd have something to tell me that I didn't already know."

"Different kind of problem, and another one down at one of the drill pads. You didn't hear?" Joe asks.

"I'm listening. Go ahead. Tell me what you need," David says.

Joe looks at the gun rack at the back of the room. In addition to the two rifles displayed on the rack, David has a handgun on the shelf in a box. Guns became their friends; he doesn't know exactly how that happened, but it did. They love them, clean them, protect them. He doesn't need the guns today; he needs something softer and more difficult. He needs understanding, he needs persuasion, he needs influence.

"No, David, it's not like that. We've got vandalism at the drill site, at the compressor station, and at the waste storage area too."

David watches him, waiting.

"They've got something in common," Joe says, and he comes close enough to David to share the pictures that he saved on his phone.

Joe scrolls through them. They look at the evidence together.

"Down at the station, they thought it might be the twins. I don't think so. They go down there, you know, Mark and Matt. They shouldn't, but they do. I keep telling them not to. Too dangerous," Joe says.

He shows David a photo of graffiti at the drill site, another shot of a defaced water tanker.

"Can't be them. Look at it," Joe says. The tanker is sprayed with acid in patterns of fiddlehead fern leaves with unfurling hands and fingers. Where the acid ate through the paint and dripped down the steel, it left rusty trails. Reminds Joe of dried blood. All of the images are drawn, painted, or sprayed in a distinctive artistic style. Joe feels alternately fascinated and repulsed by the pictures.

He stops at another image, of a fly with a horse head. He wonders what David will think of the drawing. To Joe, it looks like a mythical beast.

"Mutants, strange-looking. We got an artist, then, don't we," David says. Coldness creeps up his fingers to his hands and forearms. He knows this particular drawing style all too well.

Joe nods. He scrolls to more of the photos. One is a shot of Beth's student portfolio cover, *Chimera Me*. The pages of her art project follow, one after another. The drawings are the same subjects and style as the graffiti. Flowers, leaves, stems, sprouting with or connected to isolated human body parts: hearts, lungs, kidneys. Apart from scale, they are nearly identical to the graffiti. The last one is a bluegill fish with hands growing out of the sides as fins.

"Creepy," David says.

"Your Beth's final project for Muriel's class." Joe is unhappy to say it. "She didn't show it to you, I expect."

"Didn't know she'd finished."

Joe rubs his eyes with his hand. "Looks like she's doing a kind of protest there."

David raises his eyebrows and grimaces.

"Remember when it was just the power lines they were putting up out here? What was it, forty years ago?" Joe asks.

David laughs, "God, it *was* that long ago. Over forty years. What, I'm fifty-six now and I was a teenager. Seems like yesterday." He feels the warmth returning to his body and a flush in his cheeks. The visit isn't about a crime. It's about a friendship.

"They all got so upset," Joe says.

"We did," David says. "But you were in the city then, right?"

Joe nods. "I heard about it. People here were thinking those electric power lines gave off radiation."

"They do. That hum, that vibration, that's the electromagnetic radiation." David says.

Joe shrugs. "Maybe it is. Probably so. People thought it killed the cows. Kids slashed tires, if I remember right."

David shakes his head slowly. "We did. And then I got the leukemia all those years later. So there it is."

"You're still doing good. Strong."

"Not like I used to be, Joe. Not at all." David thinks about how completely his life has changed. After the chemo, he can't have any more children. He knows he'll die of cancer. Everyone dies of cancer here. Joe moved up here; maybe he'll be alright. But all the people born here who stay long enough to die here. They die of cancer.

David goes on, "I remember when the power lines went up here. We were...violated." He thinks about how they looked like iron giants, monstrosities. "God, how we hated them. It wasn't like we didn't want progress or anything. They were making us sick, making our animals sick."

He remembers that whatever they did to protest, nothing made a difference. They slashed tires, then construction workers got new tires. The energy company kept on putting up power lines for the city. They were relentless. "You can't do anything about money like that. Nothing at all."

Joe says, "I don't know. What works? Now, take Vietnam, what the monks did there. That worked."

"Lit themselves up," David says. He grimaces and rolls his eyes.

"Burned to death," Joe shakes his head.

David nods. The thought of bodies burning makes him acutely uncomfortable. He's seen places burn and he's seen people burn too. "Not effective in Tibet, though, not yet. Maybe it won't be either, not ever. I don't know."

He recalls the news reports, over fifty self-immolated; monks, students who burned themselves to death in the Amdo province. The way he sees it, outsiders came in and ruined their land, ruined their lives. He thinks they need their leader back and their land to themselves. Not exclusively the monks, the students and the farming people suffer too. Nobody comes to help them out over there. He reads about it and though he's not a sentimental person, it tears him up. He can't understand why that occupation doesn't end.

He says, "Maybe it's not what you do, but the time, whether it's time for a change."

"Has to be the right time," Joe agrees, "and you need a leader."

"But this thing we've got here, this gas drilling, it's different. Something else entirely. It's not *oppression*, not technically, but it *is* really oppressive. They come here, and the drilling's killing us from underneath, destroying our future. And maybe Beth's right, that it's somehow making...mutants out of us. We can't do a damn thing about it, nothing at all. Turns me inside out, Joe, I mean it. Pissing into the wind, if you even try to talk about it here. Most people won't do that much. Who can you even talk to?"

"We're talking about it."

"What's the point? Can't do anything to stop it."

Joe stiffens. "I live up here now. I ought to be able to do something about it."

The two men stand together silently. David wonders whether his friend would actually do something, if that something were against the law. He expects that he would.

"I don't know about the gas drilling," Joe says. "The government tells people that the shale gas will get us energy independent. You think so? Free of foreign oil? Well, if it did, we could get out of the Middle East."

"It won't."

Joe nods. He expects that David is right. He's usually right; he knows his history and he keeps up with his reading.

"You can't use gas to run trucks," David says. "You can't use gas to power ships either. No. Transportation's still going to use oil. You know it will. That's the biggest part of what we need. So we'll still be fighting for oil. If not oil, then whatever else the powers-that-be think we need over there."

"Heard that the big bank started mining gold in Afghanistan now," Joe says.

"I read that. Goddamn banks."

"They had an exhibit at the Metropolitan Museum of Art there in the city, all that gold from Afghanistan. *Hidden Treasures from the National Museum, Kabul*—now that was impressive. You didn't hear?"

"Heard. Didn't go."

"They had a beautiful gold crown," Joe remembers. It was something from another world. The nomad crown had gold trees around the top, tiny leaves and flowers suspended dangling from them. The piece was very natural-looking. "They got it for the exhibit, excavated from a tomb at Tillye Teppe."

"Where's that?" David asks.

"Not far from Sheberghan, in the north."

"Shebergahn...by Sheberghan Prison?"

Joe nods. He's certain that David knows this was the location of the first US casualty in Afghanistan. It was during the Battle of Qala-i-Jangi.

"Maybe your Beth would have liked it, that exhibit. Maybe not." Joe remembers being at the museum and how he kept thinking about the Afghans as he walked through the exhibit. He even thought he saw them. Their bodies seemed to be there, looking out at him from under the glass in the display cases along with their things. They were pressing their hands up against the glass from the inside. Trapped.

"It was a beautiful place. Rich, the center of the world. One time, anyway."

"Back before Alexander went and invaded it," David says, agitated. "That's why I didn't go see the exhibit. You want to think about it like that? Like a museum? I don't."

Joe rocks on his feet. "I thought I saw a dead girl under the crown, with the crown on her head as if she was alive. Not real, a...what do you call it..."

"Hallucination," David says.

"Something like that. They took that gold crown off the princess' head—skeleton I mean—during the excavation. There's a picture of it, part of the exhibit. It's gross. I didn't enjoy myself, not really. Dead people all over that exhibit. Ghosts. That's their history, their gold. I don't get why people have to bring it over here to a museum. It's not ours."

"Art appreciation. I expect you saw the piece online about resources they've got mapped out all over Afghanistan now?" David asks.

Joe says, "I did. Oil maybe isn't even the half of it. That whole situation disturbs me."

"We went over there for that."

"I didn't."

"I meant, that's why they sent us. No disrespect."

Joe holds his head up high. "Well, now I'm back. I'm just trying to live clean and simple. I've got the organic garden going out behind my place for the seventh year. Did you know?"

"Seven years, that's the tipping point for perennials." David brightens up. "Really, it is. By seven years the roots get set in, they get adapted. That garden means a lot to you."

Joe smiles. "It does. I don't put any chemicals on it. Do the whole thing myself, every year. The berries took off this year. And you know how that takes five years just to get them going. Asparagus is spread out now. They come back stronger every year. I've got so much asparagus this year; I don't know what to do with it. Took some over to Matt and Mark so they'd have some green stuff."

David nods. He appreciates Joe's paternal instincts.

"I got to liking asparagus now." The feathery fronds of the new leaves remind Joe of Beth for some reason he can't identify. Maybe because of her hair. He shakes off the thought.

"I put in tomatoes, eggplant, peppers for the summer. I put in a plum tree. It does mean a lot to me. Plums—I even put in fruit trees."

"I know you did."

"I wanted to go natural. Go organic, I thought. Go clean. The only clean food is stuff that I know where it comes from. Was I an idiot? Now I've got no good water anymore. I'm asking myself how the hell I'm going to water all my plants this summer. I'm on the water tanker, like you are. We don't have water for plants."

"Sucks."

"Even if I do water it, what about the stuff that comes up under it, from the groundwater? And the spring; there's that too. It all comes from the same place. The place they're drilling. And they take most of the water. What the hell am I going to use to water my plants now?"

"We could get rain." David shakes his head. The coldness creeps in again, from his shoulders to his neck.

"You saw the dead circles on Frank's lawn at the end of the road?" Joe asks.

"I did," David says. "Those plants are dead. I saw the brown circles all over his property. His place is done for." The cold reaches his gut and he shivers. He wonders whether his place is next, whether Charlotte's herb garden will die, whether her roses will turn brown.

Joe says, "I think it comes right up out of the ground, not just through the pipes. Kills the grass. Are we on our way to a desert wasteland here, like where they drill in Texas? I don't want to live in a place like Texas. Or like oil fields in Iraq and Afghanistan. It didn't seem possible to me before. But all the signs are here now."

"The brown circles—that's the methane from the drilling. It comes from the explosions where they're fracking the wells. Methane doesn't all come up through the pipe if they hit gas there. Some of it goes through all the cracks in the rocks. It comes up wherever it can. Gas doesn't know a pipe from a crevice or a stream. It'll come up in the pond, in my water well. Gas wants out and it comes out. Kills everything, kills anything. They get some of it into the pipe if they're lucky, but the rest of it...you know how gas is. You can't control it. Not at all. The same problems we had guarding pipelines over there. You can't control fuel. No one can," David says.

"Oh! Hey, you heard about the well that caught fire?" Joe asks, but he knows David did.

"Still burning."

"And the water here, I can't drink the stuff anymore. It's brown. It burns. I drink the bottled water. But I bought the place when I came up here because it was clean." Joe practically spits the words out.

"It was a great spot, Joe, it really was. We had paradise. We threw it away."

"What the hell. I should've stayed in the city. You think?" Joe asks.

"No. No, I don't. Don't think like that. We need you up here. Get your water tested," David says. "You saw what came out from the health group, from the doctors?"

Joe shakes his head.

"You didn't hear? Get it tested. Test for chloride, sodium, barium. You have to test it. Do it now, and then do it again, regularly."

"I will. You tested yours?"

"It went bad, you know it did."

"Okay, I get it. I know it's disturbing to have the gas drilling going on here. But about these pictures...Look, we can't have the kids going down to the drilling sites. Kids are vulnerable. They're still growing. The health problems are worse for them. You know that."

David nods. Of course he knows. But he also thinks that Matt, Mark, and Beth are old enough to make their own decisions, whether or not the choices they make are dangerous.

"If we can keep the kids away from the drilling..." Joe's voice breaks. "I don't have any of my own. I keep telling the twins, but they don't listen. Keep your daughter away from it. Don't let her go down there. I'm asking you."

"I heard you. I'll speak with her. I have to tell you something about that snapping turtle I mentioned, the one in the pond. That thing came out today for the first time. Ever. Christ, I don't know what could have been in the water to make it come out. Right up onto the dyke, and Beth was just standing there looking at it."

Joe raises his eyebrows. He wonders what could have made the turtle surface. Methane, possibly.

"I shot it. Hell yeah," David says.

"One shot?"

"In the neck."

"From the house?"

David nods.

"Damn."

"I have no idea how long that thing was down there," David says. "I won't let anything happen to Beth. She's my daughter, my angel. You know that."

"She is."

"Come on." David walks Joe to the study door. "Let's get a drink."

"What a day. You heard about the accident this morning?" Joe asks.

"Around here, wasn't it? They closed school early," David says.

Joe nods. "Route 32. Traffic was blocked off for a while. You should have seen the chaos. All those trucks and nowhere to go. The school bus got bumped by a tanker. Your daughter didn't tell you about it?"

"She doesn't talk much. That's not a bad thing, if you know what I mean."

"The bus turned over. The kids are alright but Nan DesChamps' dead—heart attack."

David stares at his friend. Old Nan DesChamps taught him history in high school. He loved history. She played the organ in church for the choir since he can remember—probably fifty years. He loved the organ music. David knows he's always the last one to hear gossip and he wonders why. He thinks maybe Joe will want to talk more about what happened, but he's not sure. Joe already talked a lot more today than he usually did, and he's clearly disturbed about Beth's drawings.

"Scotch or brandy?" David asks. "Charlotte's got both in the kitchen."

They pass by the table and Joe stops to look at the almond cake. "She still acts French out here in the middle of nowhere."

"It may be the middle of nowhere to you, but to her, no. This is where she grew up. This is where she raised our child. This is the center of the world," David says seriously.

Joe nods.

Beth breezes past them through the room. "Going riding," she says.

The two men watch her leave.

7 PM

Adrian gets out his bicycle and heads over toward the house he and his father stopped at earlier in the afternoon. He's curious. He can't keep himself from thinking about that family: the superhero man, the ethereal girl, the sensual mother. He rides along the edge of Smith's Lane where not much traffic passes by him, but he stays away from Route 32. The air seems clear and the last rays of sun stream through the trees around him. The tree branches look like they are dancing.

He's in love with Brindle.

He sees someone riding horseback in the field near the edge of the forest. In the magical hour when the sun is falling down behind the trees, the sky is pink. He thinks that to live up here in the country must be like a dream, a good dream. The horseback rider approaches the road and he recognizes her, the girl from the house. She gets down from the horse and walks, holding the reins loosely.

"What are you doing out here on a bike? You don't drive?" she asks.

Adrian shakes his head. He lost his license months ago for a DUI offense. He certainly doesn't want to talk about that.

Beth thinks he must be younger than Matt and Mark, who drive already. She looks over Adrian's bike. It's silver and seems new. She imagines that he must not ride very often. She watches him get off his bike and wheel it along beside her.

"You don't have to go to school?" she asks.

"I've been out for a while," he laughs. He doesn't think it should matter that he's older, and he wants to spend time with her without scaring her away.

"What do people do here in the summer?" he asks.

She shrugs. "Normal things. What do you do?"

What he does in the summer isn't different from any other season, now that he's out of school. "I don't know. Visit you."

She smiles at him; she likes the idea. "I do the regular things—ride, hike. And I meditate. I do yoga. I swim. We have a stream back there, behind us, past the trees."

Adrian thinks he'll walk to the stream later and see where it leads, maybe try hiking. He's never been hiking. He needs to find himself.

"Mostly I draw. Maman sings," Beth says.

"Your mother?"

Beth nods. "She writes stories and songs. Different people do different things."

As they walk along together, Beth picks chamomile leaves and clover flowers. They grow wild by the road. These and purple asters, even wild roses flourish here without any cultivation, perfectly harmonized with the land. The wildflowers have grown in these fields for countless generations.

"My Da builds houses and things all year. Some of the guys come help when school lets out. They work summers." She puts the flowers in her pocket.

The twins drive by in their pickup truck and beep. Beth looks up.

Mark leans out the window and hoots at her, "I love you!"

She waves at them. "Like those two," she says.

"Friends of yours?" Adrian asks. He recognizes them as the ones who pushed him around at the scene of the accident this morning.

"Kind of, but they're too old for me. They're twins. They'll work with my Da this summer again, probably. They graduate this year." Beth releases the horse's reins. Jolie wanders under a maple tree and nibbles at the wild plants.

Beth picks a large pink clover flower. She sucks on the base of the florets, one by one, pressing them between her teeth. "You know how to do this?" she asks.

He shakes his head.

Beth hands him one. "Try."

He bites the end of the flower. It tastes bitter and he makes a face.

She laughs. "It's sweet, if you don't bite it. There's nectar inside; that's why the bees like them," she says. "You suck on them. Flowers make sugar from sunshine and water. Photosynthesis—it's kind of magical. A circle: sun, water, plants, and then sugar."

He notices the clusters of heart-shaped, bright green leaves beneath his feet. "That's clover, right?"

She nods and plucks leaves from a tall, blue-green plant growing by the side of the road.

He notices the triangular leaves have a powdery white surface that looks like miniature water droplets reflecting light. "What are those?" he asks and watches her.

He thinks she seems to float when she walks, like some kind of wood nymph. He guesses she can't weigh more than a hundred pounds.

"Lamb's quarters, we call them," she says, "because of the shape of the leaf. Like a wild spinach kind of a thing. Good for health, Oma taught me."

"Who?"

"My Da's mother. Oma. Her people come from here, way back. She's a healer. She was, anyway, back when she could talk."

He raises his eyebrows.

"She lost her voice. Now I'm learning from a book, *Indian Uses of Native Plants*. Just to keep up on that part of my learning. I could teach you about the plants while you're up here. If you want," she looks at him sideways. "If you don't have a lot to do, I mean."

Beth plucks a stem of lamb's quarters and hands it to him. "Try."

He slowly chews and swallows a leaf. He's surprised to find that he likes it.

"Oma says, when we were put on earth a really long time ago, each person came with a plant to heal all the troubles that come later." Beth watches him process the thought. "We've got Indian balsam, sage, wild rose. We've got juniper berries and honeysuckle. All of them do something different inside, heal things. And you know, we have plenty of troubles up here."

Then Beth falls silent. She would like to ask Oma more about the old stories—how she learned to be a healer. She thinks about the heritage project due for history class this week. Oma would be the perfect one in the family to tell their story.

Oma is a mystery. She's darker than Da, and when they visited relatives out west in the Dakotas last year, Oma's brothers teased her about her hair. Beth loves Oma's thick hair. She would like to ask her more about her side of the family. She can't now. Oma never talked much before, and these days, since Cherrie died, she doesn't say anything at all. She lost her voice, but some of her knowledge lives.

Beth remembers some of what Oma taught her. She thinks it was not nearly enough. She learned mostly from what Oma showed her by doing things, more than from what she said. They would walk anywhere, everywhere, fence or no fence. Nothing could stop Oma from going where she wanted to go. She knew where to collect the right roots, leaves, and flowers for tea when one of them in the family was sick. And she knew mushrooms in the forest and roots in the field that were good to eat. It drove Maman insane to think of Beth collecting wild mushrooms by herself, for fear of being poisoned. Oma collected wild plants everywhere, on any land, and no one minded. If they did, she would walk right up to them and talk about the land, the plants, and the family. You could not be irritated with Oma.

When the energy company came and the gas drilling started, things began to change. The machinery was big, the people that ran it were foreign to the area, and the balance was affected. Oma stayed inside more. The sacred link between Oma and the land seemed broken. Now Beth remembers what she can and tries to make her own connections.

"Let's sit down," Adrian says to Beth. They find a soft dry spot under an oak tree away from the road.

She jumps right back up. "You stay here," she says.

She runs off and he watches her go. She reminds him of a wild animal—a little fawn possibly. The afternoon heat is rising off the field in waves that make the horizon wobble. *A mirage*, Adrian thinks. The scent of grass and clover is strong and sweet around him.

She comes back panting and carrying a handful of leaves and flowers.

"Close your eyes!" she demands.

He does.

"I'm going to pinch a leaf and you guess what it is."

"How will I know, if I can't see it?" Adrian asks.

"By how it smells, silly." She presses a narrow, blue-green leaf and holds it right under his nose.

"Perfume."

"No. What plant. What kind of plant is it?"

"Right, flower perfume," he opens his eyes.

"Lavender. It grows along the edge of the field," she says.

"Wild?"

"No, the family planted some. It keeps coming back more every year."

He puts the bruised leaf in his mouth.

"I wouldn't—don't eat it. You make tea with lavender. Or pillows; sometimes we make little pillows for sleep. Close your eyes!"

He does and waits. Beth picks out a tiny yellow chamomile flower bud. It is no larger than the nail on her pinky finger. She crushes it between her thumb and fingers and holds it under his nose.

"Shampoo," he guesses.

"Plant!" she insists.

"Daisy or...no, something woody." He tries again. "No—what they make tea from...?"

"Chamomile," she says and drops the flattened blossom into his hand. "Makes you sleep. Chamomile is like a sedative. But it's legal."

He opens his eyes. He pushes the yellow particles released from the center of the flower around in his palm and puts it in his pocket. "Yes, Sleepy time tea. I know this one."

She hands him a sprig with small round leaves, "You'll know what these are too, I think."

He sniffs the leaves. "Candy. No, just kidding. Mint, right? Spearmint?"

She nods. "You can eat them. They're fine just like they are," she says and pops three leaves in her mouth. "They're good for you, good for everybody."

"All these grow wild here?"

"In the summer they do. We live in a kind of heaven, you know." She sprinkles leaves and flowers in a semicircle around them. "Where'd you think all your tea and soap and medicine and all that stuff comes from? You don't know, do you?" she laughs. "Oma taught me where to find them—right here."

Jolie whinnies and stomps her front feet. Beth knows the time has come to head back home.

"Close your eyes," she says to Adrian.

"No."

"One more time."

He shuts his eyes and leans back. Beth inches closer and brings her face next to his. She flutters her eyelashes on his cheek. He is smiling.

"Butterflies," she whispers, and her breath smells of mint.

When Adrian opens his eyes, she is on her horse already. He scrambles to his feet. "Wait! What's your name?" he calls to her.

"Beth. How long are you up for?" she calls back.

He tries to follow her. "I don't know. Don't leave me. I don't want you to go!"

She smiles at him. "That's the best part. Isn't it? Leaving something when you want more?" She rides off toward the house at a gallop, leaving Adrian alone.

He picks up his bike and wheels it back to the road. He wonders why she would think that leaving someone interesting is a good thing.

***

Beth settles Jolie back in, at home. She shovels out the stall and gives her fresh hay. She brings water from the house for Jolie and watches her drink it, but she's thinking about the new boy with the bike.

Back inside, Beth runs up the stairs and sifts through the papers in her room, looking for her drawing pad. She has to finish the family heritage project, but she has some time. She would need to interview one of her parents for that. She sits on her bed, drawing a circle of wildflowers.

Da approaches the door of Beth's room. His feet are heavy but something in his heart is light, quivering. He was surprised that he wasn't angry about the graffiti. The sensation he has is hope, he thinks. Pride too. He feels an unexpected pleasure in the idea of his daughter making an anonymous public statement with her drawings.

Did she realize what she was doing?

The light is on in her room and the door is open a few inches. Da hears the faint scratching of her charcoal. She is humming softly. The melody is unfamiliar to him.

"What, Da?"

He slowly opens the door and stands in the doorway. "New song?"

"Yes, Maman's new one." Beth wonders whether she should ask him about the history project now.

"Officer Joe came by," Da says.

Beth nods and looks up from her drawing. She knows; she saw him before she went out riding. She waits. Officer Joe doesn't bother her. He's a friend of Da's and she believes he is a good person. Sometimes he and Da have a drink together. Other times he only comes to pick Da up, and on those days they leave quickly with their guns.

Da says, "People made an issue out of something they found over at the drilling site. And the compressor station, too."

"What about?"

"Vandalism. Graffiti."

"Oh!" She covers her face and laughs silently.

He knew it was her without having to ask. "I saw your art project."

"You did? I didn't get to show you. I handed the pictures in today. Da, I'm sorry."

"He has them—Joe does."

Beth frowns. She puts her drawing pad aside and stands up. "Why? I just handed them in. He's not supposed to have them."

"I mean, he's got photos of them on his phone. Don't worry about that. But the other thing, people are upset about it. What it means."

She shrugs. "I draw what I see."

Da wonders what she's seen that he hasn't.

She remembers the fish kill, and later, the fish she found with the tumor growing out of the side of its body. She closes her eyes and sees the mutant butterfly she found with the ruffled wings and short antennae.

She says, "I draw what I see in my mind. Not really real, but feely-real. What things look-like-feel-like."

Da can't think of anything at all to say to her for a moment.

"Well, you keep at it, then. Fine drawings. Seems like you have a gift," he says and walks away, satisfied.

"Da?"

He turns back to her.

"Da, how old were you when you met Maman?"

"Oh, I was a lot older than she was."

Beth watches him, smiling.

"I was forty-one." He wants to ask her why, but keeps the thought for another day. He remembers that his daughter is now the same age that Charlotte was when he discovered her. Thirteen.

Da suddenly feels terribly old.

8 PM

Dusk gradually covers the hills with shadows that move forward in waves, advancing faster than Adrian can bike. He's on Smith's Lane, on his way back to the house that his father rented for the week. Adrian hadn't thought about what biking here would be like after dark. In Brooklyn, the streets are always well lit. The streets are never completely empty there, although they are quieter after two in the morning. Here in Brindle, he's surprised that no streetlights are installed on any of the roads. At only eight in the evening, the area is utterly abandoned.

He feels like the trees are stalking him as he passes them, moving up and down in the shadows with each push on the bike pedal. He knows this must be an illusion. The moon has come out and as it gets stronger, it seems like the half-open eye of an enormous beast, watching him, following him. He is afraid.

He bikes under low-hanging tree branches and a tiny black bird flaps erratically right in front of him. He pulls away and skids sideways, falling off the bike. The creature glances his cheek, whisper soft. It's not a bird. He thinks it might be a bat. It flits past again—a bat for sure. He didn't think a bat would come so close to a human, not in real life.

He's left the countryside dream and entered a wilderness nightmare.

Adrian picks up his bike and gets back on, riding faster. He hears an owl hoot long and low, a sound he's never heard before in nature. Dogs yip from somewhere in the hills behind him. He wonders if they are pets or wild dogs. One lets out an extended howl and then he is certain that they are wild.

A few miles down the road, Matt and Mark are driving along slowly in their truck, in no hurry to get home.

"The science guy at the accident this morning—what does he do here, anyway?" Matt asks.

"I don't know. He's a scientist. Looks at things," Mark says.

"Does he know what they are?"

"No. I seriously doubt it."

"Science is about facts."

"Not really."

"No?"

Mark explains, "Like, I'm here, working right along doing something boring, something repetitive. I'm peaceful. I'm steady. Then, say, maybe you are a psychologist, and you look at me. I feel you looking at me. I tense up. I look at you. I say, 'Are you lookin' at me?' with an attitude. Because I'm pissed. I don't want you to look at me. See? Maybe you would say, well, I'm a nervous, confrontational person. But I'm not, generally. I'm more or less peaceful. So it's not just facts. How you look at it matters."

"But Mark, he's looking at the water."

"I know he is."

"The dirt, he puts it in little jars and things. It's not looking back at him."

"He's also looking at us."

Matt nods.

"And you know, he works for *them*."

"Of course he would, wouldn't he?"

"They pay him."

"I know that. Somebody has to be paying him if he comes all the way out here in that fancy car and rents a place. Who rents anything out here? No one, that's who."

"So that means something. It matters about that, about who pays him."

"Does it mean something to you?"

"What?"

"Who pays us?"

"No. But David never asked us to do anything wrong."

"So, maybe he's different."

"I don't know. Could be, could be."

They see the bike on the road ahead. "I'll be damned," Mark snorts. "The fool, you see that?"

"Want a lift?" Matt calls out the window.

Adrian is flooded with relief when he sees the truck stop. It idles beside him. Then he recognizes the twins and his heart sinks.

"Sorry about this morning," Matt says, leaning out from the passenger seat. He gets out of the truck. "Didn't know you were a friend of Beth's."

Matt helps Adrian put the bike in the back. "I'm Matt. He's Mark. Free advice for you, Romeo: Don't ride that bike after dark here. Not if you want to stay alive."

Adrian agrees. He's happy for any human company at all right now. "Thanks. I'm Adrian," he says and gets into the truck.

Mark asks, "You bring anything up with you from the city?"

"The bike," Adrian says.

"Nothing, like, recreational?" Mark asks.

"Weed, that's all." Adrian reaches for his front jean's pocket.

Matt stops him. "No. Don't even think about it. You can't light up out here. We'll drive down past the four corners. We know a place that's safe out there. It's not far."

They drive a few miles up a hill and pull over. The young men sit and smoke together on the hill overlooking a valley. The area is sparsely populated;

only a few homes are visible below them. Adrian thinks the house he's staying in with his father might be one of those lighted buildings down in that valley, but he's not sure.

"I'm starving," Adrian says.

Matt and Mark look at each other but they don't respond.

"Are you guys hungry?" Adrian tries again, thinking that he may just have to go home.

"We're not eating," Matt says.

"Not for a few days," Mark adds.

"What about drinking?" Adrian asks.

"No, man. We're driving. Are you crazy?" Matt is insulted.

"Right. Why aren't you eating?" Adrian asks.

Mark says, "It's like this. Sometimes our clothes don't fit. You know?"

Adrian looks from one brother to the other.

"And we don't want to buy clothes," Mark goes on.

"No money for it. Spending money on clothes is kind of stupid. So we don't eat for a few days," Matt explains.

"Then the clothes fit," Mark finishes. "Always works. I don't get why people buy clothes all the time, anyway. Such a waste of material. You know what else I don't get? Why people diet. They eat special food and call it dieting. All you have to do is stop eating. What's so hard about that? Tell me one person in the history of the world who stopped eating and didn't get smaller. One. You can't. Can you?"

"So, you guys are fasting?" Adrian asks.

The twins nod.

"Intermittent fasting," Matt says. "That prevention guy talks about it."

"The doctor," Mark adds.

"Never heard of it. Fasting is impossible for some people," Adrian says. "Don't your folks try to get you to eat?"

Matt and Mark look at each other.

"We don't have folks," Matt says.

"Right." Adrian wonders why. He thinks he should leave that comment alone. He doesn't know anyone his age who doesn't have one or the other parent, or both, around at home. He lives with his mother in Park Slope and visits his father in Bushwick. Both neighborhoods are in Brooklyn. Living alone would be out of the question for him now.

Adrian looks up at the night sky. He marvels at the view as it gets darker and the planets and stars start to become visible. The night sky is beautiful here with no city lights competing with the heavenly bodies. He's never seen anything like it. He tries to remember what the constellations are supposed to be from his trips to the Natural History Museum planetarium. He sees the Big Dipper but he can't pick out anything else.

"God, it's amazing," he says.

"Billions of stars, if you come out late enough to see them. Midnight is good," Mark sighs. "Billions. Trillions, maybe. Who knows?"

"So, Adrian, what's your old man do in Brindle?" Matt asks.

"I honestly don't know; it's the first time I've been up here with him," Adrian says and laughs.

Matt and Mark share a serious look.

"You don't know what your dad does?" Matt asks.

"It's not a secret or anything. He works here sometimes. He's a scientist. I know what he does—he analyzes things. I meant, I don't know *a lot* about what he does."

"Maybe you should find out," Matt says.

"It's crazy, when I think about it. I went to Bronx Science and I don't even know the details about what he does out here."

"Interesting," Mark says. He knows smart kids here would do anything to get away. To have a chance to go to a specialized high school like Bronx Science—that would be a dream come true.

Matt says, "Can you imagine if Beth could go there? God. That would be something else. Maybe she'd be a doctor."

"Something to think about, Beth being a doctor. I'd go to the doctor if she was a doctor." Mark stops, lost in the thought. "Guys, want to head back?" he asks.

"No. But yeah," Matt says. He nudges Adrian. "Let's get going, Romeo."

"It's Adrian."

"I know, but I like calling you that," Matt says.

They slowly move back to the truck. Adrian notices a faint glow behind the hills as if they were close to the city. They aren't.

They drive off slowly with the windows open and now the night air is getting cool. The lights behind the hill grow stronger. A noise that started out like a hum gets progressively louder until it sounds like a jet plane and shakes the air continuously. The ground vibrates. Adrian tries to imagine how that would sound in a song. Apocalyptic, he thinks, if the sound was done as a droning pulse behind the voices of the singers.

Matt and Mark put up the windows. Adrian thinks they're driving toward his father's rental place. Instead, they make a turn and go up a steep hill in the forest. They pull over beside a clearing. Lights illuminate a cluster of tall white tanks. Beside them are rectangular basins of water. They are as big as Olympic swimming pools.

"What is this place?" Adrian asks.

The brothers share a look. They didn't think Adrian had been up here before and they were right. "Drill site. They're drilling for gas here," Matt says.

"Right," Adrian says as if he should know, but he doesn't.

"Fracking," Mark says.

The twins get out and Adrian follows. The noise from the machinery is deafening.

Mark yells, "Come on, Romeo; we want to show you something."

Adrian follows them. The area is marked with No Trespassing signs. Given the overwhelming odor here of acids and fuels, he's sure there is a good reason for keeping people out of the area. Pipes crisscross their path. Yellow and black hazard warnings surround the perimeter. The twins don't seem to notice at all.

Trucks pull in behind a drilling rig.

"Goddamn trucks," Mark says and he kicks the dirt in their general direction with his heavy boots.

"What happened to the truck driver after the accident? Do you guys know?" Adrian asks.

The twins look over at him.

"The driver," Adrian repeats.

"Police have him. He's screwed," Matt says. "We thought you were one of *them*, this morning. Like I said, I'm sorry about that."

Mark says, "You know how many truck trips it takes to get all the water and chemicals up here to frack a well?"

Adrian shakes his head. He has no idea. He hates the trucks too now. Watching vehicles pull in, he thinks of the children sitting by the school bus, crying. He remembers the girl pointing at the driver slumped forward motionless in her seat. He shudders.

Mark continues. "I can tell you. I counted. Two thousand truck trips for every time they frack. That's a lot of trucks. That's a lot of exhaust. That's a lot of air pollution."

"We're all screwed," Matt says.

Tanks stand above them like great illuminated giants. Adrian thinks of Stonehenge. That place had a purpose, a long forgotten one. He imagines that the stones were placed in harmony with the earth, the seasons, the sun, and the stars for a reason, possibly to help the civilization plan for planting and harvesting.

As they get closer, Adrian notices that the sides of the tanks are covered in graffiti. Leaves, stems, flowers are combined with human organs and body parts like hearts, eyes, fingers in overlapping outlines. He stops and stares, trying to distinguish the forms.

"That's her work," Matt says.

"Whose?"

"Your new friend Beth Smith, Romeo. She paints everything around here. She'll paint anything that's not alive," Mark says. "Maybe she'd paint something alive. I hadn't thought about that before. I wonder if she'd paint me. Anyway, wanted you to see it. She's special. She knows about the plants, the stars. Not a witch exactly but—"

Matt interrupts him, "Like a good witch."

"Yeah," Mark nods seriously. "She's like, some kind of goddess."

Matt says, "That's it. Or the daughter of a goddess, maybe. She doesn't belong in a place like this." He flinches and rolls his shoulders, to shake off the feeling of missing his mother. It always comes over him when they come up here; he's not sure why. He feels like the place is some kind of purgatory.

"She's showing us something," Mark declares.

"I know she is. Look at it," Matt says.

Mark goes on, "Your old man works here, just so you know. It's a dirty, dirty place. You couldn't pay me enough to work here. Never. It's hell on earth. I'd rather be dead and in real hell than work out here while I'm still alive."

Matt looks around him at the bright lights and tall tankers. He feels like he could be imagining it. He never comes up here unless Mark insists, and then there is nothing he can do, but go. "You sure we're alive?"

Mark bends down to the ground. He takes a cigarette lighter out of his pocket.

"No, don't do it Mark!" Matt yells.

"I want to show him. He has to see it," Mark says.

Matt backs up and covers his face with his hands. Mark flicks his lighter beside a puddle at his feet. It ignites. Flames flare around Mark's boots all the way up to his knees. He jumps back. The three young men silently watch as the fire burns. It slowly dies out. The puddle has vanished.

"That wet stuff there? Not water. It's some kind of lighter fluid, like what's in the one I've got in my hand and you've got in your pocket," Mark says, pointing to Adrian's front jean pocket. "It's got lighter fluid inside. But here, we've got lighter fluid outside. Any kind of fire here is like flicking the lighter. We're all like one big lighter now, without the plastic container around us. That's why you don't light up in some places. So we don't explode."

"Don't do it; don't light up out here," Matt adds. "Don't even think about it."

*****

On the drive back Adrian is silent. Smoking always makes him anxious, and after the night bike ride, the bat, the dogs, and now the fire, he's terrified. He points to the turnoff for the rental house when he recognizes it. They pull the truck over in front of the house. The place is brightly lit on the inside. The policeman's vehicle is in the driveway, parked behind Henry's red electric car.

Matt gets out and helps Adrian with the bike.

"Your old man's home, Romeo."

"Adrian."

"And you got company."

"Right. Thanks for the ride," Adrian says.

Mark leans out the window. "We know where your old man works. Now we know where you stay. We know where to find both of you. So watch it with Beth," he says.

"If you do anything to hurt her, "Matt adds, smiling, "we'll kill you."

Adrian believes that they actually might.

9 PM

A Luna moth the size of Beth's hand rests motionless at the top of her kitchen doorway. This is a rare sighting; usually Luna moths come out only in early summer, and never in the house. The pale green wings are transparent and even thinner than silk. The eye patterns on the wings are blind but Beth can't stop looking at them. The large antennae are feathered, like a white comb, to pick up scents from far away. She knows the moth will live for only about a week and won't even eat, not at all. Finding her love—a mate who may pick up her scent from miles away—is critical now for this beautiful creature that rests on the door.

Beth tries to think up ways to get the moth back outside. She intends to keep the Luna moth's life cycle unbroken.

The front door opens slowly and Beth looks over. She hears Maman say goodbye to someone, and watches her head straight to her bedroom. From the wave of heavy perfume that reaches her when Maman walks by, Beth knows they've been drinking. Extra perfume doesn't cover the fact, but confirms it. She is disappointed about this. She waits a few minutes and then follows her mother.

"What happened?" Beth asks, standing in the doorway.

"We went out. It was Sara. She needed to talk to someone," Maman answers.

Beth walks in slowly and looks around. The photos of family—some from long ago—cover a wall. One of the pictures in an ornate oval frame is of eleven sisters with their hair up in loose buns. They wear frilly blouses and long skirts. The sisters sit together smiling for the family portrait. Another tintype photo of Great Grandfather sits on the desk. Beth wants to know about all of these family members, to know each of their stories.

Maman explains. "They wanted to have a child. Sara and her husband. You know?"

Beth shakes her head. She didn't know.

"But now she's been poisoned," Maman says.

Beth is stunned. "What from?"

"Ah, you know. Their well went bad; it's been burning. Now they have poison in the water. Phenol, the doctor told her. I don't know what that is. A toxic thing—oh, don't ask me. She's been very sick." Maman begins to cry. "She's ruined...their family is ruined..."

"Come," Beth says, and she takes Maman's hand. "I want to show you something." They walk together and Beth stops to show her the large moth. "Look at this, Maman. Isn't she pretty?"

Maman's head is swimming, but she tries to bring the object on the top of the doorway into focus. Pale, mint-colored, long, eyes on its wings. She recognizes the Luna moth.

"Oh! She has to go outside before it's too late," Maman says.

"Yes, she has to go outside."

"She's only got a week."

"I know. She was probably attracted to the light. Let's go out too and visit Jolie—want to?" Beth leads Maman, supporting her. "We'll turn off the light, leave the door open for the moth, and maybe she'll find her way outside behind us."

They walk in the dark to the barn behind the house. Jolie is quiet in her stall.

Beth takes Maman's hand and places it on the velvety soft nose of the horse. She watches the life of the horse flow through the touch to Maman as her crying stops. This always helps. The transfer carries Maman back to the world Beth understands, this world.

"Jolie," Maman says. She is remembering to love, to care. "She got out today?"

"Yes. We went for a ride." Beth pats the horse's neck softly in gratitude. *Thank you, Jolie.* When she pulls her hand back, it is covered with short hairs. Jolie has started shedding. Beth frowns, remembering her science assignment where she learned that one of the toxic chemicals was related to hair loss.

"Tell me a story. Tell me a story about the family, Maman," Beth says. "I have to write a paper for tomorrow."

"For what?"

"History. A paper on heritage. You'll help me with it, won't you?"

Maman's face brightens. "Of course! Da and I named you Elizabeth. This means God's promise..." She tries to focus her eyes on her daughter's face.

"And I am your only child," Beth finishes for her.

Her mother smiles at her. They walk back in the darkness to the house, talking. Beth opens her laptop at the table and they sit side by side.

"Your family came from France, long ago," Maman says. "You still have family there, you know. If you ever have to leave, you can go to them. They're in Marseille, in the city. And we have a genealogy. Do you know where it is?"

Beth shakes her head.

"*Mon Dieu*, where can it be? Ah, never mind. Our family, on my side, goes back to...William the Conqueror." She watches Beth type. This beautiful girl is the future of the family. She thinks it is about time that Beth had a boyfriend.

"He was a bastard," Maman whispers.

Beth covers her mouth with her hands and laughs. She loves it when Maman is in a mood to tell stories.

"Not a bad man—no, I didn't mean that. But, you know, his father wasn't married to his mother. So, he was a bastard. Doesn't matter. You see, because of him they spoke French for three hundred years there, in England, when William was king. That's why we have so many French words in the English language."

"Yes, and you speak French."

"*Oui!* And my parents and grandparents did too. But I also learned in school. I learned to read in French. They don't teach it anymore at school, do they?"

"No, they don't teach French, Maman. I will try to learn in the summer. And long ago, we were rich?" Beth asks.

"Some of the family had land and houses. You don't notice now, because we don't spend the way most people do. We don't show it the way Americans tend to do—money, I mean. But we don't have to look for it either. Not a good thing or a bad thing, but that's how it is with us."

"When did they come here?"

"Hmm," she hums and tips her head sideways. "We came in the late 1600s, with the army. They were all Catholic, you know. One of them came accidentally. She got on a ship for a party. Some party! They were sailing for the New World and didn't tell any of the women, because they needed more women here. But after they were so far out into the ocean, what could the kidnapped women do? They had to come. You still have family there...Beth, do we have any more of the brandy?"

"No, Maman. No more brandy." Beth knows her mother is expecting, but not how to protect her from herself.

"Ah. I'm not supposed to drink. The doctor said drinking is forbidden in my condition. What can I do?"

"Don't drink then. It makes you sad anyway. Have tea. Would you like me to make tea?"

Maman nods. "You know, the family came from Louisiana—New France, as it was called. They named it 'new,' but it was not new. Thousands and thousands of Indians lived there, so many more than French. And this is how your family got to know about the land here, the plants and the flowers. We learned about using them for medicine and food. We learned the magic in them. Yes, dear, it was many generations ago, very long ago."

"That area isn't French now."

"Napoleon, you know. Napoleon Bonaparte, he sold it. The French owned Louisiana and then he sold it. I would say he was a fool to sell it, but who can say Napoleon was a fool? You still have family there too, you know. In New Orleans you have a very large family. Your great grandmother was one of eleven sisters, all of them beautiful like you."

Maman walks into her bedroom and returns with the black-and-white portrait of the eleven sisters in the pretty oval frame.

Beth smiles at her and continues typing as Maman tells each of their stories. She falls silent.

"Why do people sell their land, Maman?" Beth asks.

"I don't know. I really don't. Money, I suppose. Money and hope. People have hope. They hope for something different, something they don't have. I have what I want. And so the idea of something different doesn't have an appeal, not for me. But, you know, Napoleon, he did sell New France. He sold it to the Americans. And you see, don't you—then we were called Americans. Not a very nice name, not pretty, but I suppose we're stuck with it now. This was a very long time ago."

"When?"

"Hmm, I think...1800 or so. That's how it was. They came here and they bought this land. They planted the pine on the hill, you know? And now it's become a great forest. And they started the lavender that runs through our fields. Ah, I love it here, Beth. So beautiful, all of it, isn't it?"

"I thought you planted the lavender."

"Some of it, yes. What else? Let's see...your father, Da, he builds, of course. His people were here long, long ago—the Smiths—then they went out west. They were farmers, I believe, but he's a builder."

"And Oma?"

"Oma's side of the family is from here, from way back. Before the French or the English came, your Oma's family lived here. Then they were forced off their land and had to move out west. Didn't she talk to you about them? Before, you know...before we lost Cherrie, before Oma lost her voice?"

Beth shakes her head. "Not so much." Oma was not fond of conversation, not ever. She didn't talk much and she really never listened to anyone about anything—not as far as Beth remembered. She taught Beth about the plants by demonstrating.

"When you were a little girl, you experimented quite a lot. This did drive me crazy. Really, it's miraculous you never got sick," Maman laughs.

"One time you sat in the vegetable garden eating rhubarb leaves. This was before you could walk. I found you and lifted you up out of the rhubarb patch. You're supposed to eat the stems, you know, not the leaves. They're poisonous. I think it was because of Oma always showing you the wild things. You ate a few different poisonous plants by accident. But not when you were with Oma. She would never let you make a mistake. Oh no, she protected you."

Beth thought Oma's family roots in the west were Native American. Like the quiet and magical forest, Oma's origins were hidden and treasured in Beth's heart.

"She is a mystery," Maman whispers and she leans to the side, her head in her hands.

"And you, Maman. Talk about you."

"Me, nothing so much to tell. I had you when I was still a girl. I studied French and literature. I like to read and I *love* music. I write poems, songs, as you know. I sing about the things going on around me here. I have a new one about the columbine flowers, you know it?"

Beth nods. "The new song is so lovely."

"So, that's me. And I'm awfully tired. So very, very tired now. Did this help? You must finish school. You will, I know it. God's promise..."

"Of course, yes. I'll write it now, Maman. You sleep."

Maman leaves the table slowly and goes into her dark bedroom without turning on the light.

10 PM

"I was shocked. Stunned, really." Henry is reeling from the events of his day. He sits drinking on the couch in the rental house.

Officer Joe is visiting. He sits across from Henry in a wing chair. The windows of the house are open. A cool breeze moves past the two men and disperses the summer heat that was trapped in the room. Joe's known Henry for years, a neighbor from his old place in Brooklyn. Joe had to see him tonight, in person, to make sure he didn't run back to the city in a fright after the school bus accident. Henry is a cowardly sort of person. Yet he has something that Joe wants, advice. And he wants it sooner rather than later.

In the summer, Joe relies on his organic garden for most of his food. He's uncertain as to whether he should any longer. He's not sure that the food grown here is safe, not anymore. He expects that Henry can help him with that.

Henry says, "That truck hit the bus this morning, and I felt like the world was coming to an end in front of my eyes. Children. Why did it have to be a bus full of children! And then the tanker, *God!* That could have leaked. It was wastewater, which is still toxic, but it could have been fuel. Exploded even. Can you imagine?"

Joe has seen many explosions before when he was in the service. "The kids had scratches, bruises—nothing terrible, really," he says. "Not physically, anyway. Except the boy who saw the driver die. He's still upset. I expect he'll get over it."

"She died? The bus driver died?"

Joe nods. "Weak heart."

Henry gasps and covers his face with his hands. "Oh, no. The little boy, he'll be traumatized."

"Probably not." Watching Henry, Joe thinks it's possible that this is the first time he saw someone die.

"What happened to the guy driving the truck?" Henry asks.

"Two of our boys got ahold of him," Joe replies with a frown—"Wasn't pretty. Lost a few teeth. Now he's down at the station for a while. They're asking him some questions."

"Good. How did it happen?"

"He was smoking. Driving is tedious work. He uses recreational drugs. Coping mechanism for him, but not a very good one if you ask me." Joe sighs deeply. "It could have happened to anyone; it was an accident."

Henry nods, quite sure this is true. "He's not from here?"

"Most of the guys who work at the gas drilling sites aren't. They're from other places, like you are. I expect you already knew that. People living here, we're told about the jobs. That's in the advertising part of the operation. The jobs aren't really for us, though. We're fools if we think any of this is in any way for us. We're in their way—that's all. They're clearing us out. Like a war tactic."

Henry nods. He taps his fingers on the chair, searching for the historical reference. "Poisoning the well."

"That's right. Like I said, a war tactic. Kill the people, make them weak, then move in and take over."

Henry repeats it in his head: *poisoning the well*. He knows that the phrase means more than poisoning people physically, but the other meaning escapes him.

"I have to say, Joe, that fracking is terrible work, disgusting work. The smell, too—oh God, the smell! You need biohazard suits, gas masks. And the noise, the noise is horrible. You've heard it, right? When they do the fracking part of the operation out here?"

"Heard it. Felt it. Breathed it. We all have. That's what makes me think they're trying to get rid of us. When the drilling's done, no jobs are left. No people out here. Little solar grids on top of the pipes. Pipes sticking out, all alone out there sucking the fields dry, but not a man in sight. They leave us here with the little warning signs to keep out—the ones no one pays attention to anyway—even though they should."

Henry wonders why Joe stays. "What do the people who live here say about all of this?"

"Everyone's concerned, at some level. Some people speak out, they join groups. Families, women with kids, or folks who are planning a family, they're the most worried. Myself, I moved here because I thought it was clean. I'm not the only one. People who make it—financially I mean—they come up and buy a house and some land. Used to be, anyway. I don't know why anyone would want to come here now. They'll probably move to Maine now, or Canada maybe. Activists come here. Chain themselves to tractors. Videotape it. Artists come up here from time to time protesting. Actors, writers, anyone with an artistic temperament, most of them are horrified by the whole business of the industry. Made a movie about it—*Gasland*. You saw that?"

Henry nods, "The documentary."

Joe goes on. "Changed the way I thought about it. The thing is, most of us here haven't decided exactly what to do. We will. Maybe we don't want to be against something. We want to be for something, positive. One thing I see here is that people will support something. They'll accept it. Work hard on it. But getting people to say they're against something is more difficult. Rubs them the wrong way. Like gossip does."

"I don't get it." Poison in the well, *poisoning the well*, Henry repeats to himself. Where has he heard this phrase used before? It means something, but he's not sure what.

Joe thinks of his friend David's wife, Charlotte, who he knows has had so many problems. "If you want to say something about a woman out here, who is in fact a bad woman, what do people say? A neighbor might try to find something good to say. Like maybe, 'it was good to see her at the store last week; she's doing better' or, 'nice to hear her at church; missed her voice in the choir. She's getting out again; that's good to see.' Something like that. They might talk about how her family is doing, kids or whatnot. You see what I mean?"

"I do—saw one this afternoon. What a mess." Henry shakes his head, remembering Charlotte's change of heart about him during his trip to her family home.

"That's what I'm saying. You talk like that; you call someone 'a mess.'"

"No, I didn't mean her. *I* was a mess."

Joe isn't sure what that means, but doesn't want to know either. "They don't say things like that here so much. The way they talk, negative isn't in their nature up here. Protest is a foreign language. It seems like a kind of performance, like theater; it's not real to us."

Henry laughs. "Exactly the opposite of how we are in the city. We're against everything, all the time. Protest is our way of speaking. Pipelines are bad, smoking inside is bad, controlling any of the above is bad. It's the way we talk; it's the way we think. Performance is everywhere, from the minute we wake up and take the train to work to the time we fall asleep at night."

"Well," Joe says, "Out here they tell stories, write songs. People go to church and sing. People make things up, some of them, and others, they sing or they pray. Tell them a good story, something they can get behind, and they might like that. Like the story of clean energy, clean gas, like that. It's a good story, even though it's probably a lie. They're not about to go start a war over it."

"Thank God," Henry says, without thinking. Part of his brain lights up. He remembers the reference he was searching for, "I've got it! *Poisoning the well*. I know where I heard it. In journalism—wait, no, in logic—I'm not sure which one it is. You destroy an argument before it's even presented, by painting a certain picture, one that people can't forget. Like the picture of clean energy. That's it! They're poisoning the well.

"No matter how many facts you present, the idea is already settled. You can't argue against it, because everyone believes the story that natural gas is *clean*. They see that picture in their mind and they hear that phrase like a refrain: *clean energy*. They've poisoned the well. Ha!"

Joe narrows his eyes, looking at Henry sitting right here getting drunk on the sofa. *What a waste of intellect*, he thinks. At the very least, it's a waste of an education. He's known Henry for about twelve years and still doesn't know what to think about his friend.

"I want to ask you about something. It's about my garden. You know I have the organic garden. I think about the water—what's in it, I mean," Joe says.

Henry blinks at him expectantly.

"Would you come out and test it?"

"You filed a complaint?"

"No."

Henry thinks for a minute. Why wouldn't he go test it? He shouldn't need a filed complaint; he should go and help his friend out. "Of course, yes. Soil too, if you want, air..."

"What do you check for?"

"Hidden things, the stuff you can't smell or taste. Methane, of course, and benzene, arsenic—we test for poisons, all kinds of poisons. And radioactivity. Uranium. Radium."

"You don't worry about those poisons getting into your water in the city?"

"No."

"Why not?"

Henry looks at him and frowns. *New York City water, it's reliable*, he thinks. That's what people always say. He says it too. *It's reliable.* He stands up and pours himself another drink. He holds the bottle out to Joe.

"No, thanks. Driving."

Henry looks at the bottle of brandy. For the first time, he wonders where the product really came from. Was the place it was made clean or was it contaminated? Were the herbs added to it for flavor grown in clean soil with clean water? Was the place one where toxic industrial chemicals or hazardous waste leaked into the groundwater or flowed over the plants?

Where did the cask that the brandy fermented in originate, what wood? Was it from the Ukraine? From

Chernobyl after the radiation disaster at the nuclear power plants? Did radiation leach into the delicious liquor as it aged? Is it poisoning him now?

He stares at the bottle, terrified by his own thoughts. He's putting things in his body and he has no idea where they actually came from or what exactly went into them.

Joe says, "You're a scientist, you observe things. You're objective. What do you think about my garden?"

Henry blinks at Joe; he doesn't remember what they were talking about. "Your what?"

"Garden. My organic garden. Is it safe to eat the produce? That's what I'm asking you about, Henry. Your objective opinion. I'm asking you if it's safe."

"Oh, your garden. I don't know how objective I am, to tell you the truth." He evades the question. "They say observation changes the subject. Then you get into subjectivity. You've got your experimental scientists and your observational ones, like me...but even then, the interventions, they change things."

Joe squints at him, thinking that his friend is definitely drunk and rambling. That annoys him more than he thinks it should.

Henry leans back and stares at the ceiling. "I'll give you an example. When you put an animal in a cage, it does things it wouldn't normally do."

He is starting to think that he has been put in a cage himself, a toxic one. He has no way to get out. This cage is made of the threads that connect the elements running up from the ground through the plants and into his food and drink, flowing into the network of nerves, muscle, and bone that he relies on to get around in this awkward human form. He thinks that some of these threads are certainly toxic. He's afraid that parts of him are already poisoned, that they will break down, they will fail.

"Naturally," Joe says, and he nods.

"But people will observe, and then they'll all say it's objective," Henry says, and he's sure that he is anything but objective at this point. When he drinks, he knows that he becomes confused and emotional.

"I see your point," Joe says.

"It's really an experiment, though, if you put a cage around something that was free. Even a plant. It changes how they grow. And animals, forget it. Take tupaia."

"What?"

"Take tupaia, small primates, tree shrews. Adrian's mother—you remember Janet—she used to work with them."

"Is she still living in the city?"

"She is. Park Slope."

"See her?" Joe asks.

"No..." he can't get into that, not tonight. "So you put them in a cage, the tupaia, and then they're different."

"How?"

"Eat their own young, things like that. Really different."

"No!" Joe grimaces.

"Yes. They do. Janet was raising tupaia in the lab. They gave them the big cages, three feet by four feet, and the animal is small, like the size of a squirrel. If you leave them in pairs, then you can't get there quick enough to save the newborns before they get eaten. You come back in the morning and you can't tell which one of them was pregnant, and there are little tiny body parts all over the cage. Disgusting, really."

"Who eats them?"

"The tupaia."

"No—the mother or the father?"

"The mother."

"That's odd," Joe says. "Unnatural."

"Yes. Well, I don't know. We have our myths too, that bit about eating the offspring. I forget who. Cronos or Saturn, maybe. Anyway, the cage does it to the animals, you know. That's what's unnatural. They wouldn't normally do something like that. Self-defeating, killing off your kids. The species wouldn't survive, as a whole."

"Henry, you're a disturbed person."

"Absolute opposite of evolution, a dead end. But I have to tell you, Janet raised one of them herself."

"The little primates?"

Henry nods. "I visited it at the lab, way back when. That baby tupaia would curl up in the palm of her hand and roll around, go upside down. No bigger than a newborn kitten. Janet hand-fed it some kind of formula from a syringe, like it was a baby bottle. Added honey to it."

"She saved it from the parents?"

"I don't know if I would say that—saved—because it was still a miserable life being in a cage. Then it starved to death anyway."

"How did that happen?"

"She had to go away traveling; she had a speaking engagement about her experiments. And the staff didn't feed the baby. They eat crushed fruit, the tupaia. I don't think anyone wanted to bother with feeding the little one, going to the trouble of crushing the fruit and putting it in the cage. And when she got back, it was dead."

"That must have bothered her."

Henry nods slowly. "It was a real shame. Traumatic, I think. She stopped working with the tupaia after that. And she never wants to be two steps away from Adrian either. She doesn't trust him with anyone. I mean, he's too old to stay home all the time now—he's nineteen—but she doesn't like to see him go. Not at all."

"The way you talk about it, Henry, I could see why Janet wouldn't want you to raise Adrian."

"Yes, I know. I'm cold. I can't help it," Henry says, and he remembers what Charlotte said about him: *fairly disgusting when you talk about your work*. He knows that's true. He even disgusts himself.

"Am I disgusting?"

Joe clears his throat. "No. Not particularly," he says, but he does find Henry's stories upsetting.

"About my garden, the plants there, what do you think?"

Henry blinks, looking at him. "Joe, what happened to you out here? You're different now."

"Maybe I am," Joe says. "I got more concerned about the environment. All about being green. Did you know that the people here have a constitution? It says something like, *people have a right to clean air, pure water, and the preservation of the natural, scenic, historic environment.* I imagine that the animals and plants here, they have the same rights too when it comes to that. They need clean air, pure water. What do you think?" Joe knows he has a right to clean water. He's not sure about what Henry believes. "Not everyone agrees."

"I don't know," Henry says. *Water, clean water...*he remembers Adrian singing. "So, you leased your land, like the rest of them? Is that what you're telling me?" Henry can't believe his friend would have done that, allowed drilling under his country place.

It's been a long day and Joe knows he's talking too much, but he's not ready to leave yet. "Mineral rights— yes, I did." By nature, Joe does not regret anything, but this decision he definitely regrets. He beats himself up about it regularly. "I'm ashamed to say it. I did not know then what I know now. That's not an excuse, but I didn't ask the right questions. Let me ask you something now: Why would the water that's deep down be dirty? It doesn't make sense to me. The rock, the dirt should filter it. It should be pure."

Henry snorts. "It isn't. Opposite of pure, if anything. When you go far enough down into the earth, the environment is like the idea people have of...hell. It is Hades, I think. The concept, the myth of hell is somewhat correct. I don't know how they would have known, but the core of the earth is molten rock. And spouting steam...that's down there too. The energy companies tap it; it's geothermal energy. Radioactivity is from down there. Uranium. Radium. Radon. They go after that too, for nuclear energy. The energy business is terrible, when you think about it. That's where it all comes from. Hell."

Henry stops. He's frightened himself. He remembers what the spiritual visionary, Wallace Black Elk, a Lakota said—man's *scratching of the earth* causes diseases like cancer. He meant the mining and drilling for coal, gas, oil, uranium. The scratching brings up the things deep in the earth that should have stayed down there. Henry shudders.

He takes a drink and goes on. "If we get our energy from hell, then I don't know what that makes us. Devils, maybe. Demonic, certainly."

"Radiation's not manmade?"

"No, no more than diamonds or gold are," Henry scoffs.

"I did not know that," Joe says quietly.

"No one does. Who thinks about where radioactivity comes from? No one. We buy all this stuff, we use it, and we have no idea where it comes from, originally, I mean. No one thinks about it much. But it's all down there. We kick the people who live above it off their land, we mine uranium and bring it up and concentrate it, the same way we do with anything else, even gas.

"That place up on the hill, they move more than three hundred million cubic feet of gas a day. That's a lot of gas, a lot of money. We have to purify it to use it, but we don't actually make it. What do we really make, anyway?" Henry confuses himself with the question. Hazardous waste comes to mind—we make *that*—but he doesn't want to say it. He sits back down on the couch heavily.

"Maybe we shouldn't be drilling for it here, then. What do you think?" Joe says.

"I agree with you there. What's been down under rock for hundreds of millions of years should stay down. No one has any idea what the surface of the earth will look like if we keep on dragging that stuff up here. We're going backwards in time, back to when this place was a godforsaken rock with no life on it whatsoever."

Henry's head swims. He thinks he should stop talking but he can't. "Hiroshima and Nagasaki gave us a pretty good idea of how bad it could get."

"The atom bomb," Joe says.

"There you go. You see? Radiation is so incredibly dangerous. Deadly, lethal, and you can't control it. You can't measure it. People haven't even imagined the kind of hell we could have on earth. Not yet, they haven't. You know what's down there in the deep, deep water? Uranium-238, radium-226. These are radioactive isotopes that come up. Fracking brings them up to the surface. And the explosions blast all the toxic slurry in, to prop open the cracks in the rock. So that's radioactive material coming right back up here at us. Right back at us." Henry repeats the thought to himself: *right back at us*.

He can't stop. "We shoot the fracking chemicals in—I couldn't even tell you the list of what's in them, you wouldn't believe me—and they shoot right back up."

Right back at us. "But worse, at least forty of the things in there that we know of—and we don't know all of what's in it—cause cancer. And the water purification systems we have? They can't get rid of it. No, they can't. Uranium, that's alpha radiation with a half-life of...I don't remember what the hell it is. It must be over four billion years. We can't measure it in the wastewater, in the drinking water. And you know what's really absurd? We don't even try."

Henry stands, staggering. He pulls a device from a shelf and grins. "Most people can't, but I can."

Joe looks at the box. It has a meter on it. "What's that?"

"Geiger counter," Henry says. "Measures radiation." It cost him a few thousand dollars. He thinks it was well worth it. He uses it all the time.

Joe looks at the box carefully. He thinks he will have to get one of those for himself.

"So, my garden out back—can I find out what's in the plants?" Joe asks.

Henry plops back down on the couch. "All of it? No, you can't. Not everything. But some things you can."

"They test the food that's in the grocery stores with that thing?" Joe asks.

"Food?" Henry shakes his head. "No. All that advertising and packaging about organic and natural, that has no meaning at all." *No meaning at all.* Like Henry himself; he thinks he has *no meaning at all.* "Means nothing. Maybe the grower didn't put toxins in his vegetables and on his fruit trees or in his beef. But the environment did. The soil did. The water, if you can even call it that, the water did. That's all in there. And we eat it." *No meaning at all, no meaning at all.*

Joe is quiet, thinking about what might already be in his body from eating contaminated food. He looks at his hands, holding them out in front of him. He feels suddenly uncomfortable.

"To tell you the truth, Joe, I'm afraid to eat most of the time, unless I'm already drunk." Henry stares at Joe but can't bring him into focus.

Joe wonders if this is why Henry drinks.

"You should think about moving. Do you think about it?" Henry asks.

"Sometimes. But back to the city? I don't think so. Where would I go?"

Henry shrugs. "I don't know, and it doesn't even matter. But not here. Not where they're drilling. Not where they're dumping either. And not where they're going to drill, or going to dump. Don't go where Keystone Pipeline from tar sands is going to run, oh no, and don't go anywhere on the Marcellus Shale either. You look it up, map out the sites. It's all there, all on the Internet. You just go and have a look."

Joe says, "I don't want to leave. People aren't going to leave their homes because you tell them there's something dangerous there that they can't even measure themselves."

Henry blinks rapidly, looking at Joe. That's one of the things people always say. *People aren't going to leave their homes.* But Henry has to convince him. He has to. The idea of proving to Joe that he should move consumes him. Joe has to move! For once, Henry urgently wants to stop spouting what he knows and to say what he feels.

"If your house was on fire, would you stay inside while it burned?" Henry asks.

Joe glares at him. Such a stupid question.

"Your house is on fire, Joe. And you're still inside. Get out before it kills you." Henry leans back and exhales deeply. That should do it. He feels exhausted. *Get out*, the voice in his head repeats. *Get out before it kills you.* And now he wants to sleep.

Joe is quiet for a while but then says, "It's not even me I think about most of the time; it's the young people. They'll want to have families."

"Some of them will." Henry admits. "But if I was young now, no. Or if I knew then what I know now, I wouldn't have had kids. I would not, I'm telling you."

Adrian opens the door and walks into the room. When he sees his father sitting there with the off-duty officer, he's self-conscious about being high.

"Hey, Dad."

10:30 PM

Adrian smiles and waves at his father and Officer Joe as he walks past them to the kitchen. He feels like he's starving. He's not really; he ate in the afternoon. He thinks about the twins not eating for days. What lunatics they are, strangely lovable lunatics. Adrian takes down a ceramic mug with an owl painted on it. He remembers the eerie and beautiful sound of the owl on the dark country road. The bird on the mug seems to look at him. He searches on the shelves for a new jug of bottled water, hoping to make instant coffee. Then food—he has to have food.

He hears Joe talking in the other room.

"By the time I started thinking about family, financially secure and all that, I got sent out with the National Guard. When I got back from Afghanistan, I didn't want to."

"I'm sorry. I can't even imagine," Henry says.

"I didn't have any desire to start a family after that, if you know what I mean. So I moved up here. I thought it was pure, clean, *good* for me."

Pure, clean, good for me...Adrian repeats internally. He smiles, thinking of the web of stars he saw coming out in the night sky on the hill with the twins. The stars and planets are a network of light, of connections. He closes his eyes and the words repeat in a loop: *pure, clean, good for me*.

He feels a song coming to him, one about the new place, about hope. *Pure, clean*, he thinks, and he remembers the field and the horse and Beth. He remembers the taste and the scents of the leaves. He feels the whispering softness of her eyelashes on his skin. He reaches for the mug, fascinated by the owl's eyes staring back at him.

Joe says, "I was thinking about getting better out here. I was moving to heaven. But I'm not. You know where I'm living, don't you?"

Silence. Adrian listens.

Joe says, "I'm living in hell."

Adrian drops the mug. The pretty ceramic piece falls in slow motion down past his waist, his knees, and he can't reach it in time. The mug shatters on the tile floor in a mini explosion of shards around his feet. "Damn it!"

Joe startles, sitting up sharply in the wingback chair.

Henry puts one hand on his forehead and closes his eyes. "My son..."

Joe takes a deep breath. "Henry, you're a scientist. People would listen to you. Speak out about what you know. That's what we need. The energy company, they've got their professors. They take money from the energy company for their work, their reports, their speeches. But tell me something: Where are our scientists? Who speaks for us? The engineers, the scientists, the doctors—where are they?"

"I don't know. You're screwed. The doctors have a medical gag order. The chemists, we don't work for free." Henry has an internal conflict about his job. He remembers the disdain that Charlotte has for people like him, who are paid to work on things they don't believe in at all. *Science whore*, she called him. Humiliating to think of now, sitting with Joe.

"Say something, Henry. Do it. Let people know what you know, from doing all the tests these last three months. Put it all together. I know you could."

Joe stands. "I have to go. Nearly eleven now. But think about it. You will, won't you?"

Henry gives Joe a smile curved with pain. "I'm not a very good speaker." Science brought him an awareness of poisons that are entwined in a net around him, he knows it. He can't avoid them. They're all around him and inside him. But science gave him none of the skills needed to speak. He signed a confidentiality agreement for the consulting work, of course, which could not be ignored or forgotten.

He feels like he's sinking into the floor as he walks Joe to the door. "You get home safe, Joseph." Henry says reflexively, and he leans on the wall beside the door for support.

Joe nods. "You know, they don't say that much up here. I'll call you tomorrow. Maybe you can come by. Have a look at my garden."

Henry smiles and nods. He will do it.

He closes the door and turns back to the room. He sees two images of his son standing in the kitchen doorway staring at him, glassy eyed.

"What?" Henry says. He sees twin Adrians turn and walk back into the kitchen. Henry follows, crunching over broken chunks and slivers of the ceramic mug. "Goddamn it, Adrian, why can't you pick up after yourselves?"

At the kitchen sink, Adrian turns the faucet on full. He lets it run, pooling in the metal basin. He takes out the lighter from the front pocket of his jeans.

"I thought you stopped smoking," Henry complains. His head throbs violently.

Adrian is silent. He flicks his lighter beside the running water.

The sink bursts into flames.

11 PM

"Is that why Officer Joe says he thinks we live in hell?" Adrian asks his father and he watches the sink burn.

The flames die out.

"Don't do that again," Henry pleads.

He sits heavily in a wooden chair at the kitchen table. "I told you not to smoke here. Didn't I say that? Why don't people understand what I say? *God!* You'll kill us both."

Adrian is embarrassed. "I won't. I'm sorry," he says. He doesn't know why he did it. He had to try it for himself, after what the twins exposed him to up by the drilling site. He had to show his father. He wants to hear what he has to say about it.

Henry stands unsteadily. He tries to put water up for coffee on the electric stove but spills it all over the floor.

Watching a pool of water run off the counter, he asks, "Where've you been?" He tries to clean the spill, gives up, and sits back down at the table.

Adrian takes over. He fills the coffee pot with filtered water. "Around. Went for a bike ride. Looked at the plants. Did you know chamomile grows wild out here? And lamb's quarters—"

"—to purify the land. We use them for phytoremediation at superfund sites."

"What sites?"

"Places where hazardous wastes were dumped. Amazing plants," Henry says. "They clean poison out of the soil. Isn't that something? Should have put them all over here."

"They grow by the road. They're tasty."

Henry jumps up and nearly falls. "You ate lamb's quarters?"

Adrian nods.

"*Christ*! No, don't do that. Lamb's quarters, they concentrate the toxins from the dirt. It's in their leaves. That's how they clean the land, the contaminated land. What's gotten into you?"

"Lamb's quarters," Adrian says slowly.

"No, no! You'll be poisoned," Henry says.

"Right. But you have to try some things once." Adrian tries to think of a way to defend himself. "If you never tried anything new, I wouldn't be here, would I?"

His father is silent on that point. He feels terribly confused. He needs to sleep.

"I went up to where they're drilling," Adrian says.

Henry looks at his son and tries to focus on the comment. He doesn't think it's possible to reach the drilling pads by bike from here. "You couldn't have."

"I got a ride..."

"I see. Well, yes, they are drilling near here. It's true. You shouldn't go there. Biohazards all over the place."

"They had it posted. What is it, like some kind of mining?"

Henry can't believe Adrian was up there. He wants to give him a picture of what it looks like beneath the surface. If he can only communicate effectively, he's sure Adrian will never, ever want to go near it again.

"Yes, it's like mining in a way, but different. They drill, then they turn the drill sideways. Horizontal drilling. Then they blast it open with explosives all along the pipe. Boom! Fracking. That blows the rock apart and if there is gas, it comes out. Gas flows back into the cracks, the water, the pipe, and up and out. Gas plumes go up higher than you can imagine; no one can control them. Terrible for the air. You know the idea of a carbon footprint? Think about a bomb blast crater—that kind of footprint. The gas drilling makes a big, big footprint. Like the size when a meteor lands and makes a crater. You've heard about fracking?"

He looks over at his son. "They didn't teach you about that in school?"

Adrian shakes his head. He picks up his phone from the counter and texts a friend from Bronx Science who he's sure will know: *what's fracking?*

Henry goes on. "Hell of a noise. It's like an earthquake. In fact, it causes earthquakes. We've known that for a while, a hundred years. Drilling causes earthquakes. Scientists know it. No one talks about it. The energy company starts drilling, then come the earthquakes."

Adrian pulls away from his father, grimacing. He looks down at his phone and sees his friend's response: *synonyms for fracking - eco-Armageddon / dangerous / destroying / killer / violating / community discrimination / dying.* He looks back up at this father, wondering how he got involved with all of this.

Henry tries telling a story to get through to his son. "Imagine you're ice fishing. You're out there in the middle of the ice over a huge, frozen lake. You're surrounded by frozen water. You want the fish. So you go and take out your gun, and blam! You shoot holes all around you in a circle through the ice to kill the fish. Naturally the ice will break and you'll fall in and freeze to death. Who would do that? Well, fracking's like that, except with fire, not ice. I don't know why people still go on drilling. Poking holes in the earth. It's crazy. Utterly insane."

"No, Dad, bad story. You don't make sense. I don't do ice fishing. Fracking—that's why you're here? Why we're here?"

"No. No, I don't do anything like that. I run tests," Henry says.

"Right. But what exactly are you doing here? What are you testing for?"

"Poison," Henry shrugs. He doesn't have a better word for it. "We don't have bullets for the guns; we have poison. We drill holes all around us and pump in poison to get the gas to come out of the ground. That's it. I run tests to see if what we pump in came back up into the drinking water. The chemicals, the toxins—those are the tests. That's what I do."

Adrian holds his head in his hands. "I don't get it. What I read and what I see, it's not the same thing at all. I'm starting to think the whole 'clean, natural gas' thing is ridiculous. All those ads."

"They mean that gas burns clean, once you get it out. It doesn't smoke," Henry says.

"Yeah? Well, if it was clean, they wouldn't use it to gas people to death. You know, gas chambers?"

"Different kind of gas," Henry waves his hands in front of him dismissively.

"Really? If it was clean, it wouldn't have caught fire when I ran the water in your sink. Like, gas leak—hello, explosions? We're lucky I didn't blow the whole place up. And coal? Dad, come on."

Adrian makes instant coffee for him.

Henry sighs and stares at the ceiling. "Clean coal."

"Don't be ridiculous. That's an oxymoron if I ever heard one; the two are complete opposites."

"It is moronic," Henry says.

"If coal were clean, who would use charcoal to draw black lines on white paper? And people wouldn't say things like, 'the night was black as coal'. Coal is dirty. The people making the ads must really think we're stupid, that we'll believe gas and coal are clean. What a joke."

"You did, though."

"I don't now. What about the wind? That's clean. And solar? What about that? That's clean," Adrian says. He pours his father coffee. He thinks about the ironies and inconsistencies around him and wishes they could talk when he wasn't high, or when his father wasn't drunk.

Henry attempts to drink the coffee his son places in front of him. He can't believe they are having this conversation. Between the poverty of his son's science background and the poverty of Henry's own morals, they don't have a wealth of common ground.

He hopes he is dreaming and that he wakes up, sober.

Adrian watches his father and tries to tie together the threads of everything he's seen today. The school bus, the tanker accident, the country house, the beautiful horse, the field and flowers, the drilling site, the fire in the kitchen sink—these are all connected in some way he doesn't fully understand yet. He searches for reasons a family would give up their land for drilling.

"How much money do people make on the gas drilling, Dad?"

"Here? Not much. They get maybe a hundred thousand dollars to lease the land."

"That's a fortune," Adrian says.

"Don't be a fool. I make more than that in a year. And I have for the last ten years. So you know that's not a fortune. Gone as soon as it comes in, and they don't get it every year, Adrian. They get it once. This is not like a lease, like you lease an apartment. They're taking the mineral rights." Henry drinks the coffee and is grateful to his son for it.

"Then what?" Adrian asks.

"They are forcing the gas out beneath them. They smash the rock down there, the Marcellus Shale. They're destroying the area to take it. They're ripping up the land. They're crushing the people who live up here along with it, I think. It's tragic."

"Dad, you're drunk."

"You say that like it's a crime. It's not a crime to be drunk. But I'll tell you what is a crime: what's going on out here. We're poisoning one another. For what? You think a hundred thousand is a fortune? Let me put it in perspective for you. You get the money. Then your land is poisoned. You can't keep animals or a garden. You have to buy your water. Yes, you still own the place, but they bought the rights to the gas under it. You have to sell but you can't. Or you sell at a loss. You have to relocate, rent, start over, and with what? I'm telling you that it only lasts me, or the two of us, a year. One year. So then what the hell are the families here going to do for the rest of their lives?"

Adrian thinks about the family he met today in Brindle, and is afraid for them.

"Why don't you do something? Don't you care about the people out here? I heard him asking you to, your friend the cop. Why don't you help him?"

"I am doing something. I'm working."

Adrian snorts and shakes his head in disgust. "No, Dad. I mean, why don't you speak up? Why don't you do something to stop all of this?"

"I can't." Henry is embarrassed to admit to his son that he is powerless, but it's how he feels.

Adrian slams his hand on the table. "Who's in charge?"

"No one. It's just happening," Henry moans, and he knows he can't go on listening to this, thinking about this.

"Do something, Dad!"

"I am, damn it," Henry fumes. "I come here to do something. I work. Do you work?"

Adrian laughs bitterly. "No, Dad. But I'd rather not work, than work on something like *that*."

Henry explodes. "Do you know how much money there is waiting to be made in shale? People think there's thirteen trillion cubic feet of gas in the Marcellus Shale! That's not numbers from the gas company, Adrian. That's from the US Department of Energy. The US government."

Adrian shakes his head in disbelief. "Great; now the government's in fracking?"

"Yes, no... I don't know. But we're looking at billions and billions of dollars. Now *that's* a fortune. Do you have any idea what kind of money that is? What people will do for it?"

"As many dollars as the stars...billions and billions," Adrian says. He closes his eyes.

He sees no hope in talking about it. He stands, looks at his father one last time, and walks out the back door, alone. This isn't a place he wants to be now.

He walks behind the house and thinks he'll just walk, keep walking forever. He comes to the edge of a stream. Beth's words repeat in his head: *If you follow a stream, you can't get lost. It comes from somewhere and it goes somewhere.* He decides to follow the stream, follow the water.

He thinks, *water, clean water*. Even if the sink water in the rented house is contaminated, he's certain that the running water of the country stream must be pure. He wades in the water, splashing along in the moonlight.

*****

Inside the rented house, Henry collapses on the couch. He holds his head in his hands. He's too drunk to read. After the argument and the coffee, he's too agitated to sleep. He thinks this has been the single worst day he can remember in the history of his entire life.

He gets up, looks out the window, and then opens the door. It is pitch black. Adrian is gone. He feels a sharp pain in his chest, and this time he knows that the feeling is in his heart, but not just the muscle; it is love. As far as Henry knows, Adrian is, and has been, his only real treasure in life—unexpected, unplanned, and still mostly undiscovered. But he also knows that if he goes after Adrian, he's sure to get lost in the darkness. Henry has no natural sense of direction at all, not even when he is sober, and he doesn't know how to read the stars either.

He closes the door and staggers back through the kitchen, seeing that Adrian left his cell phone on the counter. Henry makes his way to his son's room. Adrian left his iPod on the bed. Henry puts it into the holder on the desk, drops into the chair, and listens to his son's music. The new song about water plays, the one from South Africa that Adrian was singing that very morning in the car. *Water, clean water*...the tune that has been repeating in Henry's head all day, driving him insane.

He moves to the next song. *Is it true, is it over*... he hears the plaintive female voice singing and remembers the conversation with his son and Charlotte in the afternoon. Henry is afraid that it *is* over, more than he ever thought it could be.

Henry tilts forward and feels the chair sinking beneath him. He passes out on the floor.

Midnight

Adrian walks, and with the repetitive steady motion of his pace, his rage burns off. He begins to feel calmer. He follows the stream behind the rental house uphill, walking in the water, splashing along, getting wet. He doesn't care. He has no idea what time it is. The night is warm, illuminated by the moon and stars. He can make out the forms of the trees and rocks easily. Midnight, the twins said, is when the stars will be perfect. They are.

*****

Joe arrives back home, disturbed. He falls asleep and dreams of Beth. She wears the golden crown, the one with the tree ornaments on top, taken from the princess tomb at Tillye Teppe.

In the dream, he finds Beth upstairs on the second floor of a house wearing an Afghan princess dress, walking through a room filled with antiques. Carved cabinets line the walls, and the floor is stacked high with ornate carvings and gold jewelry. He tries to explain to her that these are not hers, but she doesn't respond. He tells her the gold has been stolen, but she can't hear him.

He suspects that he is invisible; he can see her, but she can't see him or hear him.

The walls of the house disappear. Wearing the golden crown, Beth walks down the narrow stairs, out of the house. Carrying a gold walking stick—a staff—she walks away through the bare fields behind the now empty house. The earth is lit by the moon. The ground is barren; the dirt packed and dry, like Afghanistan, not like Brindle. The fields turn dark.

Joe wakes, remembers his dream, and falls immediately back into a deep sleep.

***

Beth nudged the Luna moth to go outside tonight and then followed it after she finished typing her heritage project for history class. Maman and Da were arguing about something she didn't understand, something about children, about a baby. Beth thought it might have something to do with Maman's friend Sara who wanted a baby, but she wasn't sure. At times like these, Beth walks.

The delicate Luna moth has, at most, only a week to live, to be found by a mate and lay eggs. Beth lost track of the moth when a cloud passed over the moon, momentarily leaving the fields behind the house in utter darkness. She keeps walking, more comfortable outside in the peaceful night than she is at home.

She sees him.

"Hey!" Adrian hears someone call out to him from the forest along the stream. He can't see her.

Beth stands on the bank under the trees. "What are you doing here?" she calls.

"Looking for something," Adrian says. He's happy to hear a person, anyone, along the desolate stream.

Adrian follows the water where it turns around a bend. Beth continues along the banks. The stream level suddenly rises inexplicably. It smells different, faintly sweet. Adrian is surprised by how the water rushes, frothing and foaming when there has been no rain today.

He has no way of knowing the schedule of release for wastewater from the drilling operations near the stream. It flows in, unchecked at night, from hidden locations.

"Lost again?" Beth asks and she climbs down the bank. Seeing him, she thinks of Adrian as her secret discovery. He is a newfound treasure, one she hopes to hold onto, to keep in her future.

He sees her emerge, looking like a forest spirit in the moonlight. She takes his hand protectively, stabilizing him and he holds onto her tightly. They wade along together, water splashing up over their boots and onto their clothes. The spray gets into her eyes.

Adrian looks up again at the impressive midnight sky. He's never seen so many stars, a blanket of constellations. They look like a gateway to other worlds.

"What is that? Look!"

Delicate streaks of light line the sky over them.

"Meteor shower," Beth says. "We can see them all here—meteor showers, planets, constellations."

"I've never seen anything like it," Adrian says. He thinks he should make a wish, and he does—to return here another day.

"Now you have. That group of stars is Virgo, for Persephone; can you see it?"

"Yes."

"They say Zeus put these stars in the sky to remind Demeter of her daughter, Persephone. She's the one who was carried away by Hades. Remember? Hades takes Persephone, and then the earth opens and he drags inside."

Adrian remembers the story of the abduction of Persephone. "Why did the earth open?" he asks, and he watches Beth's face closely as they walk. Her expression remains calm, relaxed. He sees that she is at home here. He imagines that she is a person who could never be lost. Slight, small, yet she is able to lead him forward like an arrow shot from a bow.

"Hades demanded it; he was a big god, you know, the god of the underworld, of hell," Beth says. "It wasn't the earth's fault. And now every year we have winter. It's because her mother Demeter is depressed for half the year." She thinks of how Maman cherishes her, and can imagine the pain of that loss.

"Demeter..." he repeats.

"Yes, the goddess for the plants, fertility, you know. So the stars are supposed to comfort her."

He believes the stars are comforting, they are to him now. "I see it. That's Persephone up there. She's lying down, right?"

"Mm-hmm. And carries a staff."

"Supposed to be 3,000 galaxies just to her left, here," he points. "I learned that from shows at the planetarium in the museum. I've never seen it in nature."

He looks back at her. "Amazing," he says, flooded with an emotion he's never fully experienced before tonight. He's unsure if it is because of the painful argument with his father, or the emptiness of being lost alone in the country, or simply gratitude for the young woman beside him. He understands now why people sing.

Beth is curious about the feeling of Adrian's hand in hers. Even though she is leading him along, she thinks he is stronger, judging from his grasp. She leans in closer to him. Each time her shoulder presses into his arm, his chest, she wants to be closer to him.

She points out and names more mythical figures in the night sky. Adrian is fascinated by them. She wipes water from her face. "I'm feeling sleepy all of a sudden," she says.

When they emerge from the water, arsenic, benzene, and toluene along with other, yet unnamed chemicals enter their bodies from where their skin is in contact with contaminated stream water. The chemicals move invisibly around and through them. The foreign molecules come in from the surface of the stream water through their breath. From the breath, they cling to the soft, membranous surfaces of the lung. The chemicals penetrate the cells of their many layers of skin. They flow into the capillaries of blood that feed each cell and remove the waste of each cell, living, growing, and breathing. They touch the surface of their eyes and travel into the tiny blood vessels that are connected to their hearts.

From this efficient muscle pumping steadily, the toxins circulate to the vital organs and throughout the body. The chemicals race along in the pulsing blood from the heart. They push out to the network of nerves that lace the body in a fragile and electric grid.

Cell connecting to cell, Adrian and Beth's bodies fluidly transport the poisons alongside oxygen and particles of energy that flow continuously because they are required for life. Creator and destroyer, side by side, permeate their bodies.

Adrian and Beth cannot fight against the sluggishness that's taking control of them. They simultaneously long for sleep but can't form the words to say it. The moment they fall to their knees on the bank of the stream, they are surrounded by toxic toluene vapor which hovers near the ground in even stronger concentrations. They lie down beside the stream.

The being that was Beth and the being that was Adrian leave their physical bodies behind, as if asleep. Their unconscious bodies become progressively weaker. They lie entwined on the wet grass under the trees, unconscious. The stars become ever brighter and the night sky shifts above them as the earth moves along its course. The night passes.

Beth ceases breathing altogether. Her organs fail, kidneys, liver, and lungs. Finally her heart is unable to continue and stops beating. Adrian lies beside her, part of his body hanging onto life by a thread with slow, even heartbeats.

*****

At the Smith's home, David walks into Charlotte's bedroom and says, "Our daughter's missing."

Charlotte sits up. "She went for a walk. There was a Luna moth; she was putting it outside," she says, and reaches for her phone.

"You let her go out?"

"No. She does what she likes, David. I didn't *let* her."

David races out of the house. He checks to see if Jolie is in the barn. He finds her clamoring in her stall, pawing frantically at the sides with her hooves. He's never seen her like this. She calls to him, snorting, but he can't stay. He runs back to the house and jumps into his truck. He drives toward Matt and Mark's place.

He finds them sitting together in front of the trailer, their German shepherd Gabby lying between them. David gets out and slams the truck door. Gabby jumps up.

"Beth. She's gone," David says simply.

The twins stand together at once. Gabby starts barking hysterically.

"God! What do we do?" Mark asks.

Matt gapes at them both. "Find her. Find Beth, Gabby," he says and pulls on his boots.

The twins take off running behind the trailer; Gabby is leading the way. They know all the places Beth walks and rides. They are determined to cover every one of them until they find her.

David calls after them, "I have the truck."

"You're not going to find her that way. She's not driving."

"Matt," David yells, "Mark!"

They are already gone.

*****

At his place, Joe wakes up from a recurring nightmare. He's falling down a cliff into a raging forest fire, and the ground shakes from explosions around him. He sits up in bed drenched in sweat looking for his squad.

He hears something vibrating. It's his phone. He focuses his eyes on it and sees that it is flashing a caller ID, David Smith. Joe knows now that he's in Brindle, he's home. He opens the phone and realizes that his hands are shaking.

"David?"

"Beth's gone."

*****

When David gets back home from the twins' place, Joe is already there, standing beside his vehicle. He's pulled off the road in front of the house, waiting.

"One in the morning. Where is she?" David asks, knowing neither one of them has any idea.

Joe says, "Bring your gun and a flashlight." He remembers parts of his dream. Beth was walking in fields, but where? He can't identify the place.

David rushes inside the house to get his things for the search. He takes his handgun out of the box on the bookshelves in the study. While he looks for a flashlight, he overhears Charlotte on the phone. He even doesn't care who she's talking with now.

He leaves her there.

*****

Charlotte's call arouses Henry from a drunken sleep. He realizes that he's on the floor in his son's room. His son is gone. He gets up, walks to the main room and turns on his computer. Between the sleep and the coffee, he feels alert. He is awake.

"You can try to do the right thing. Henry, do it. Call them, tell someone. You can make a start. And then we can begin again, a new life."

"How can we? How can we start over?" he asks Charlotte on the phone.

Henry goes through the emails he'd saved from reporters who wanted to talk to him—so many over the past several months since the fish kill. He listens to Charlotte's lament in the background like a chorus.

"Adrian's not home either," he says to her. "Don't worry. They're young. You've gone out before and didn't tell anyone where you were going. Would you tell people, if you were trying to get away from them? She'll come back. He'll come back. They have to. Stop crying. Maybe they're together. I'll call you back...I will. In an hour."

Henry disconnects. He types a number he reads from an email into his phone. Even though he is still not quite himself, the time has come to speak.

"This is Dr. Henry Berger calling, the geologist. Yes, about the chemical contamination at the Marcellus Shale. I have a story to tell," he says.

Dawn

Matt and Mark have been walking for hours in the moonlight and they haven't eaten all day. They're exhausted and hungry.

"Smells sweet. Reminds me of the night I passed out, remember?" Matt says.

"Stream's high too. Cover your face with your shirt. Here, look, breathe through it like this." Mark shows him.

The twins scour the forest beside the stream with Gabby running up ahead. They hear him let out a long, mournful howl. They run toward the sound.

Gabby sits whimpering beside two bodies collapsed beside the stream on a bed of ferns. He stops when the twins reach him and whines loudly.

Mark and Matt kneel beside the bodies. Matt holds Beth's cold, wet hands, checking for a pulse. There is no movement at all; her blood is still. Mark puts his ear next to her lips and listens for her breathing. There is no sound.

"What do I do?" Matt whispers.

Mark backs away and he is screaming. Gabby runs around him in tight circles, pawing at him.

Matt feels for a pulse in Adrian's body, his hand on his chest below the sternum. "Mark! Adrian's alive. We have to take them back," Matt says.

Mark stands over the stream, screaming.

"Mark!"

He stops screaming and comes back to the bodies. Gabby walks beside him, pressed up against his legs.

"Carry them, yes. Yes, we have to," Mark says, but he is stunned. He is not himself.

"I'll go get the truck," Matt says. "Call Joe. Joe will come. He'll help us."

"No. No, don't leave me here with them. I'll go crazy," Mark says and he grabs ahold of his brother's arm. "We have to stay together."

"I'll call him," Matt dials the phone. Waiting for Joe to pick up, Matt says, "We have to bring her back with us. She doesn't weigh anything."

"I can't touch her. You do it," Mark says, and he is crying.

"I'm not leaving her here," Matt says.

"No, I can do it." Mark moans. "Bring me something to carry her with, anything."

Matt turns away on his phone, "Joe! Joe, we found them. Adrian's alive." He waits because he doesn't know how to say what seems impossible, but is true.

"Beth's dead. By the stream. I don't know. Drowned. Can you meet us? We're where the stream goes under the road by the oak...There. Yes."

Matt puts away his phone and stares at his brother.

"What?" Mark asks.

"Wait for Joe." Matt bends down and picks giant fronds of ferns. He piles them together, making a mound, and then lifts Beth's body on top of the soft bed. He covers her methodically with fern leaves.

"We're going to carry her back," Matt says slowly. "And Joe's going to come get Adrian some help. He's calling Dr. Miller; she'll meet him at the clinic and take over. She'll know what to do. She helped me. Remember?"

"We have to take her home," Mark says.

The brothers lift up Beth's body and carry her between them. Her hair falls among the curled fern leaves and her fingers extend through the plant, as if joined to it, glistening in the moonlit night.

They reach the road by the great oak. Matt and Mark are streaming with sweat. Exhausted, they lay the body down and cover it again carefully with the leaves. Joe has to come; they know he has to. They stand panting. Gabby sits beside them, silent.

"We were waiting for her to grow up..." Mark says.

Matt finishes for him, "But she didn't."

"She loved it here so much—the plants, the birds, the animals—I hope she's in a better place now," Mark says.

"Wherever it is, I hope she's loved." Matt sits and holds his head in his hands.

*****

After Joe gets the call from the twins, he can't speak. He drives David home silently.

"They found the boy?" David asks.

Joe nods. "In a coma. I'll have to tell his father. David, can you check on Charlotte and wait at the house while I go over there?" he asks.

"I'll wait, in case Beth comes back here," David says. He gets out in front of the house but he suddenly feels an icy emptiness. He looks back at his friend's ashen face.

"She's dead, isn't she, Joe?" he asks, even though he knows Joe can't answer him.

David turns and walks inside alone.

*****

Joe leaves quickly. He drives as close to the stream as he can get with his vehicle. He sounds the police siren twice when he sees the tall oak and he waits. Matt appears, haggard, his sweaty hair matted to his head. He leads Joe to where Mark waits beside Beth's body on the bed of ferns. Joe gasps. She looks like her drawings, merged with the plants around her.

"I'm going to have to tell her father," Joe whispers, looking down at her.

"First you have to go get Adrian. He's alive," Matt says and he collapses to the ground.

"Gabby! Let's go get Adrian," Mark yells.

Gabby takes off and Joe follows, running with Mark beside him.

*****

At the Smith's home, David goes upstairs to look for his mother, Oma. The room is empty. He remembers she was going to visit Sara's house tonight, about the skin problem.

He comes back down, and enters Charlotte's room. He watches her. She sits by the window at her writing desk, awake but motionless. She knows that something has happened; she doesn't know what. She thinks he may have heard her on the phone with Henry. She is afraid.

"You said you'd never leave," she says and looks up at him.

"Charlotte, I won't. But you're going to have to go away for a while, until we find Beth," he says gently.

"I have to go away?" she asks and looks at him sadly.

He thinks she doesn't recognize him, not like she used to. Something has changed; everything has changed. He knows that Charlotte is life itself, and now she has no place here. "It isn't safe for you here now. Everything is dying, but not you. You are living. You have to go. You have to leave."

He takes her by the hand and slowly leads her out to the barn. When they reach Jolie, the horse is thrashing in her stall.

"Earthquake. They get like this before an earthquake," Charlotte says.

The horse nods her head wildly, snorting.

"Yes, maybe," David says, and he helps his wife get up on the frightened horse. "It's time."

He opens the door to the stall and hits Jolie hard on the flank.

"Get out of here. Go! Go on!"

He listens to the sound of the horse hooves pounding the ground, receding, gone. He believes Jolie will take Charlotte somewhere safe, safer than here.

David walks to the barn and finds an old can of kerosene from back when they could burn, before the water went bad and methane saturated the house. He carries the can with him and climbs up to the top of the enormous pile of wood by the house. He pours the kerosene down, saturating the wood all around him.

The moon glides behind the clouds and the night is black.

He stands, takes out a book of matches from his pants pocket, strikes a match, and is immediately engulfed by the fire. He raises his hands to the heavens in supplication above his funeral pyre.

The fire ignites a series of methane explosions at the house. Flames run across the field to Sara's home and merge with fire at the water well that was still burning.

The blaze extends farther and farther into Brindle. It ignites a gas leak that explodes at the compressor station. A gas plume leaps hundreds of feet into the sky, on fire. The blast shakes homes for miles in each direction.

People wake up in every corner of Brindle. Some think the explosion is an earthquake. Sirens go off in volunteer fire stations in three towns. Men rush to respond, running from their beds to their cars and trucks. They race to sites where fires are already burning out of control, but can only watch.

Forces shock the town, forces made not by man alone but joined by the power of the depths of the awakened earth. A tremendous boom sounds; it is like nothing they've ever experienced here before. The rock layers deep beneath Brindle shift. The entire section of the continent trembles with immeasurable force. It snaps into an aberrant position, creating an earthquake centered under the place so gravely insulted by man.

*****

Joe and Mark carry Adrian between them. A fire rages behind them. Through the smoke, they can just make out the great oak and then Matt. Before they reach him, the earthquake rips through the area. Joe and Mark stumble. They watch horrified as the ground tears apart beside the road.

Matt scrambles backwards away from the chasm grasping the roots of the old tree. Beth falls, descending as if she has been claimed by Hades. Her body disappears into the darkness below.

In the cacophony, it seems as if the gods themselves sing a requiem.

Epilogue

Smith's Lane and Route 32 are clogged with a surging river of cars, trucks, bikes, and people fleeing from Brindle—the town on fire, the town that died. In the opposite direction, reporters and video crews pour into Brindle for the story. We've had fires and we've had earthquakes before, and no one responded. This time, Brindle has made the news. The media has decided to cover the story of our ecologic apocalypse.

*****

Adrian lies in a coma for two weeks, then awakens. In six months' time, when the story dies, Adrian's half-sister, Cheryl Elizabeth Smith will be born somewhere else—in Brooklyn or in New Orleans or in Marseille. I wonder whether the place she lives will have water for her, clean water. I hope that it will.

*****

THE END

Brindle 24

About the Author

J.J.Brown is the author of *Death and the Dream* short stories, novels *Vector a Modern Love Story*, and *American Dream*, and the poetry book *Natural Supernatural Love*. Born in the Catskill Mountains, J.J.Brown lives in New York City. The author was trained as a scientist and completed a PhD in genetics.

Website: Brindle24.com
Twitter: @jjunebrown
Facebook: JJBrownAuthor and Brindle24

Brindle 24